HOPE IN DEFIANCE

A ROMANCE IN THE ROCKIES NOVELLA BOOK 5

HEATHER BLANTON

Cover DESIGN by Ravven and Virginia McKevitt

Scripture taken from the HOLY BIBLE,

KING JAMES VERSION - Public Domain

A huge *thank you* to my editor Lisa Coffield, Trudy Cordle, and all my awesome beta readers!

IF YOU HAVE HOPE...

Hope Clark has fought hard to convince the town of Defiance that a woman doctor is good for what ails them. But when certain physical challenges present themselves, hard facts spur her own doubts, crushing her self-confidence. And if she can't stay, if the city is really where she belongs, what about the people she has come to love, especially a certain cowboy?

Lane Chandler's never been in love before and isn't exactly sure what his heart is telling him about Hope. After all, she's a doctor and he's just a cowboy. Or so Dr. Edward Pratt happily keeps reminding him.

Lane wonders if Hope could truly be happy practicing in a remote mining town. Pratt believes she would be more fulfilled serving in a Philadelphia hospital. With him.

In the end, nothing but true love will give Hope the freedom to choose her own path.

Please consider signing up for my newsletter at
http://bit.ly/HeatherBlantonNewsletters
to get the latest news on new releases, events, parties, and other interesting bits of history! You'll receive a FREE story for subscribing!

WHY I WROTE HOPE IN DEFIANCE

In my fourth Defiance book, *A Destiny in Defiance,* I introduced readers to a female doctor--Hope Clark. Dr. Clark is based on the real-life Rocky Mountains physician Susie Anderson. I was so intrigued by the idea of a woman serving as a frontier doctor I just had to look into what challenges a lady doctor would have faced back then. Let me tell you, it took a special woman to be an M.D. in the rough-and-rowdy West.

I wanted to write a little more about Hope and her adventures, so I hope you'll indulge my whim here.

This book is dedicated to you, my readers. Y'all are some of the toughest, grittiest "Ladies in Defiance" I've ever met or read about. You inspire me. I hope *Hope in Defiance* will inspire you to always believe in yourself and trust in the Lord!

CHAPTER 1

*D*octor Hope Clark pulled open the ash door on the stove and sighed. A few measly coals glowed in the bottom.

"Just once," she muttered, tossing in some kindling, "couldn't he get here early and warm the office?"

He being Dr. Edward Pratt, Hope's ex-fiancé and an uninvited guest to Defiance. Well, technically not a guest anymore. She was forced to share her practice with the man.

Trying not to let the current facts bother her any more than normal, she watched the smoke curl and finally, small flames grabbed hold of the wood. Pleased with herself, she rose just as someone knocked on the office door.

Wishing the patients would have given her more time to ready for the day, Hope grabbed her white apron from a wall hook and was tying it on as she opened the door.

A frail woman in a moth-eaten coat smiled at her. "Doctor Clark, I was so hoping you'd be in this early."

"Is everything all right, Mrs. Davis?" Hope wracked her brain, trying to remember the woman's ailment. No, she'd brought an infant daughter in. "The baby. She's—"

"Fine. Crawling around the cabin like an ant. I can't tell ya how grateful I am for your help. And I didn't want to leave this with anyone else." She thrust a package forward, wrapped in brown paper and tied with a red piece of yarn, and motioned for Hope to take it.

"What's this?" Nonplussed, Hope hesitantly accepted the package.

"Just a little Christmas present to show our thanks—"

"Oh, you didn't have to—"

"I know we didn't." Mrs. Davis laid her hand on top of Hope's, tears glistening in her weary, brown eyes. "But you saved little Milly's life. This don't even begin to express my thanks."

"But it's what I do."

"No, not everyone would. Coming here to this mean, cold town."

"Yes, I suppose not many women…"

"Nah, not even that. Most towns we've lived in, the boom towns are so rough and gritty, no doctor wants to come, male or female. You're right. You're here because it's what you do. Bein' a woman ain't got nothing to do with it. So," she nudged the gift, "thank you for caring."

Hope found herself at a loss for words. Mrs. Davis nodded and headed back down the snowy walkway. They were both surprised to find Edward standing at the edge of the yard, as if he'd been listening. Mrs. Davis nodded politely to him and went on her way.

Perplexed at something in the woman's comment, Hope turned from the doorway, leaving it open for Edward, and trudged thoughtfully over to the stove. *You're here because it's what you do. Bein' a woman ain't got nothing to do with it.*

The observation intrigued her. Mrs. Davis was the first person Hope could recall who saw her as a *person* practicing medicine, not a *woman doctor*—something less than a whole doctor. The distinction wasn't small. It seemed everything Hope did in her life was judged first by her gender. And therefore, accordingly, she had been held to a lower standard. Mrs. Davis saw heart and skill first, gender second.

How interesting. Hope realized she'd been beaten into seeing gender first, ability second. Obviously, such was the case if Mrs. Davis' comments were having such a profound effect on her—

"The locals paying you in gifts?" Edward asked, closing the door behind him and joining Hope at the stove. Chuckling, he peeled off his gloves a finger at a time. "A cheap little bauble they think will sway you to lessen their bill?"

Irritation climbed Hope's spine. "You're saying a woman can be swayed with gifts."

"Yes, of course. It's your nature."

She purposely bit her bottom lip to keep her mouth from running free. Edward's arrogance and chauvinism seemed to know no bounds. And not that engaging him on such matters ever changed his mind, she explained the gift to him nonetheless. "Their bill is paid. In full. This is merely a gift of appreciation."

"Oh. Well, isn't that kind?"

His cold tone, however, suggested he was miffed at not receiving one as well. Hope was tempted to offer consolation and say surely someone would give him a gift as well.

But she didn't wish to lie.

---

*L*ane Chandler, foreman on the King M, strode up to his boss's desk, pulling off his worn Stetson. Charles McIntyre looked up from his newspaper at the jangle of spurs. "Morning, Lane." His voice was thick with his Georgia accent, smooth and refined, like the man and his clothes. And that black, meticulously trimmed beard. McIntyre liked things *just so*.

Lane pulled a ledger from beneath his arm and passed it over. "Got them counts you asked for." His own Texas drawl was thicker, his grammar rougher around the edges, his clothes worn with hard work, and he supposed these differences said a lot about them. Lane was far more easy-going. Both men, however, lived for the challenge. Neither of them liked things to come too easily.

Charles took the book and began flipping through it. "How are they looking?"

"Came through the blizzard a hundred percent." Lane sat down, nearly lifted his boots to set them on Charles' desk, but remembered the boundary between friends and employers, and kept them planted. "We didn't even lose a heifer."

"That's darn near miraculous."

"Darn near. Small herd is easier to corral and bunch up, though. The test'll be next winter when the new herd is here and you're running three or four thousand again, not just three hundred."

"Yes, I suppose, but I have confidence in your abilities."

"Well, I do try." And right there was another similarity between them. Charles knew business. Lane knew cattle. They stuck to their strengths. Both men chuckled, but Charles let his laughter die and Lane caught the shift in his friend's light expression to one of sobriety. "Somethin' the matter? Somethin' to do with Delilah?" If that she-devil was around—

"No. Unconfirmed rumor—that I'm working to confirm —is she is wintering in Ruby City." Charles scratched at his chin. "This news is more specific to you."

Lane waved his hat, giving him the go-ahead to say it.

"I want to read you something." Charles raised the newspaper lying on his blotter. "From the Denver Post. 'Former

Texas Ranger Theodore Jefferys was shot and killed Sunday at St. Bartholomew's Church as he was leaving services.'"

Teddy? Lane jolted at the name of a former Ranger. A good officer and a steady friend.

Charles continued, "Witnesses said a man approached Jefferys, pulled a revolver, and yelled 'Remember Swansboro,' as he fired his weapon."

Thoughts, images, sounds collided in Lane's mind at the mention of the border town. He could still smell the gun smoke, hear the screams, taste the tension in the dusty air.

"The murderer then ran into the crowd, eluding police. He still has not been apprehended at the time of this report.

"The assailant is described as tall, slender, with dark, matted hair, and he was dressed in what witnesses said was 'worn and filthy' leather clothing. Police ask if you know anything about this case, please report to Station 14 and speak with any of the detectives."

He waited a moment before looking up. Lane felt his jaw twitch as he tried to keep from grinding his teeth.

"I take it you remember him. I knew Jefferys as well. We served together for a few months during the war. I'm sorry for your loss."

"He was a good man. One of the best Rangers Texas ever had."

Lane knew his expression must be as tight as rawhide. No Ranger should ever go out like that: ambushed.

Haltingly, Charles asked, "Lane…do you know about Stanton and Wilkins?"

"Stanton and Wilkins." He blinked, bewildered. "From my Ranger unit?"

"Yes. Did you know they are dead as well?"

Lane frowned, his gaze roaming over the richly appointed room, but not seeing the family portraits and mounted cougar. "Jefferys *and* Stanton and Wilkins?"

"Lane, three men who served with you as Texas Rangers have all been murdered in the last eight or nine months." Charles rose abruptly and walked around to the front of his desk to better see the map of the United States on the wall behind it. Lane rose to join him. "That's the only reason they were in the paper and I happened to see them. The first two, I didn't think anything of…"

Lane shook his head, staring intently at the map. "But now a third one? All killed the same way?"

"No, if I recall, one man was stabbed to death in Valdosta, Georgia. The second man was lynched in Missouri."

Lane heaved a great sigh and rested his hands on his hips. Information was coming together in his head and he didn't like the bottom line. "There's a fourth. I happened to hear Jake Farnsworth was killed last month down in Oglala. Trampled to death in the livery's corral. I thought it was an accident, but now…"

He scanned the map and thought he saw a pattern. The deaths had happened east to west. As if…he shrugged at the foolish idea.

But Charles seemed to see the pattern as well. "You could argue these deaths are connected."

"By Swansboro?" Texas during Reconstruction had been a wild-and-wooly place. With only twenty-five units of twenty-five Rangers to police the massive frontier border, battles too often had been bloody and vicious. Two units, one of which was Lane's, had only six men—men with highly specialized skills.

"Valdez should have never tried to take the town," Charles observed. "And once trapped, he should have surrendered."

Lane nodded at the common assessment of the battle. "You know it weren't us that killed him. The American ranchers went ahead of us and attacked him. We had to jump in to save their hides. Their actions didn't give us any choice."

"I know. I've read the accounts."

"But it's been eight years. Why would anybody…?"

"Lane, I'll do a little checking. Maybe these deaths aren't connected. Maybe we're seeing shadows where there are none."

"Maybe there are. Valdez had a son. He was fifteen at the time. His grandmother spirited him across the border to Mexico, but he was cursing us to hell and back as she did."

"He was a boy. His father was under siege. It's understandable, but not probable that he would carry through with the threats."

Lane chewed on his bottom lip and shook his head. He stared at nothing, yet could clearly recall the bodies of American cowboys branded to death, literally, and the ranchers' dismembered body parts hanging from Cottonwood trees by the Rio. Swansboro should have been a worthless border town except for the fact that Mexican ranchers had wanted the range as much as the Americans.

"Valdez was brutal," Lane recalled. "As bad as the Apaches for figuring ways to torture and kill Americans. His boy saw a lot of it." He blinked, coming back to the conversation. "I know where a couple of others from the unit are. I'll send some telegrams, tell 'em to keep their eyes peeled."

"You think there is anything here?"

Lane shook his head, pondered the deaths. "Mighty strange coincidences, and when it comes right down to it, I don't think I believe in 'em."

"Then you keep your eyes peeled, too."

***

CHAPTER 2

ope kicked at the snow, several inches deep, and sent up a glittering cloud of flakes to scatter in the breeze. The snowfall in Defiance was beautiful but the hem of her dress was going to be soaked and she tugged it a little higher.

"I shoulda made you ride on Copper," Lane said, walking beside her as they crossed the street.

Hope cut her eyes to the handsome cowboy, taking in his rugged, earthy appearance. He was frowning down at her, disapproval etched in his wrinkled brow, glimmering in his hazel eyes. He pushed his hat back a hair and his expression softened. The straight, blond locks surrounding his face danced in the wind. "I mean, your feet are gonna get cold."

"I think I can manage a walk to the telegraph office and then to the restaurant without succumbing to frostbite." Especially considering the late afternoon sun was sitting low in a cloudless sky. The day was not frigid, merely cool, and there wasn't even a hint of more snow.

"Yeah, speaking of dinner," Lane dragged a hand across his freshly shaved jaw, "Tell me again why I am doing this."

She stepped up on the boardwalk, swept free of snow, and released her dress. "Edward calls it a peace offering. He has asked Lucy to prepare a very special meal for us—paid her handsomely for the trouble, I might add—and wishes to offer it as a token of friendship. He feels you and he got off on the wrong foot."

"'Cause of you." Lane's lips slid into a sideways grin.

Hope had to laugh. "Yes, because of me. But he says that's all in the past now and wants to build a more cordial relationship with you."

Lane sighed. "Wants to bury the hatchet," he mumbled, but then lifted his voice, "Long as he don't want to bury it in my skull, we'll be fine."

Hope stopped and took Lane's hand. "I have to work with him, until such time as he goes away. I'm convinced he'll leave soon. In the meantime, I'm hoping this dinner might help Edward to…" She struggled for words. "Be more amenable. His bedside manner is stiff, to put it kindly."

She could tell Lane wanted to offer all kinds of comments based on the twisting of his mouth. Instead, he scratched his eyebrow and motioned down the walk.

---

*L*ane was only a little surprised to find the hotel's dining room empty—except for one table covered with a white tablecloth and set with sparkling china. A warning bell rang somewhere in the back of his mind. He smelled a rat.

"Oh, my," Hope whispered. "Looks like Edward was quite serious about a special meal."

Lane looked down at Hope. Underneath her cape, he'd seen flashes of a blue silk dress. And her glistening, auburn hair was up in a fashionable sweep held by gold combs. He touched the old, black string tie at his neck. Underneath his sheepskin coat, he was wearing fresh duds but a wash and a lick-and-a-pat with an iron didn't dress him up enough for this event, he suspected. "Yeah, it looks pretty fancy."

He took her coat, peeled out of his and hung the garments on the rack by the door. He turned back to Hope, and the pretty picture she painted about took his breath away. Slender but curvy, petite but not too short, she filled out the gown nicely and the blue of it seemed to make her eyes and skin glow. The winter breeze had kissed her cheeks with an adorable blush, and Lane reckoned right then he could eat dinner with the Devil himself if Hope was sitting beside him.

"Lane, are you all right?" she asked, the blush in her cheeks brightening.

Though he didn't think he could tell her any of his fool-ish, romantic thoughts. Not in gushy words, anyhow. "Counting myself lucky, was all. You sure are a picture."

Suddenly bashful, she lowered her gaze and smoothed her dress.

Resigned to the good and the bad of the evening, he offered his elbow and escorted her to the table. It sparkled warmly from the candle burning in the crystal centerpiece, its light dancing off dozens of pieces of cutlery. *Where did they find all that silverware?* Lane wondered. And why did they need so much of it? He counted only three settings, but each had multiple plates, saucers, glasses, cups, and utensils.

"Hope, Lane," Edward called coming from the kitchen. Lane braced himself and looked up. The man was strutting past the tables, sure enough, in a tuxedo. Did he actually travel the country with one?

Edward extended his hand toward Hope as he brushed a rakish, blond curl from his forehead. For effect, Lane guessed. "Thank you for coming, Hope. My, the gown is lovely. You are a portrait waiting to be painted."

Hope smiled, politely, Lane thought, but without much warmth. "Thank you."

"And, Lane," Edward turned and offered his hand. "I am so glad to see you accepted my invitation."

Yep, Lane was sure he'd walked into something. He shook hands with Edward, but the message in the man's blue eyes was cold, hard. "I'm looking forward to this fancy meal," he lied.

Edward stepped back and opened his hands. "You are in for a treat. Hope, I've had your favorite prepared."

She gasped. "Duck à l'orange?"

Edward's face lit up. "With savory sage cornbread stuffing, baked sweet potatoes with spiced butter pecan topping, and gingered cranberry-pear chutney. However, we'll be starting with a warm beet salad, and to finish, for dessert, we're having a chocolate mousse."

Lane's stomach growled. He didn't know half of what he was about to eat, but it sounded good. Hope touched his arm, laughing. "It should be a fabulous meal."

Edward motioned for them to sit and he pulled the chair out for Hope. "It was no small thing, I can tell you, getting some of the ingredients and this silverware delivered, but it's done, and Lucy has taken to my instructions perfectly. She has the makings of a true chef, not just a frontier hash slinger, as she calls herself."

A little mystified, Lane picked up a tiny fork and studied it. One of *three* that were sitting to the left of his plate. *Who needs three forks for one meal?* His consternation must have shown on his face.

"We've over-set the table, Lane," Edward said. "My apologies, but I though Hope might enjoy seeing a complete setting. You'll only need your dinner fork and your salad fork, oh, and then of course, the dessert spoon."

11

Lane set the small fork down, assuming it was not needed. Yep, this was gonna be a long meal.

"*H*ope, I pray you'll forgive me the wine choice." Carefully, Edward poured a shimmering red stream into Hope's glass. She bit her lip, and leaned forward, eyes wide with anticipation. She reminded Lane of a kid peering at candy in the mercantile's window.

"It looks lovely," she said, reaching for it.

"I so wanted a merlot from Château de Goulaine, but it was impossible." He poured Lane's glass, then his own and sat down. "I remembered your fondness for pinot noir from Dopff-Au-Moulin, and, lo and behold, I was able to get a crate shipped in time. Very exciting."

"Very," Lane muttered, sniffing the wine. He thought it smelled a little like peat moss. He sniffed again. Nah. Peat moss soaked in an oak barrel stuffed with raspberries.

Edward raised his glass and swirled the liquid around and around, staring into it like he expected to find something. "No doubt, Mr. Chandler, it will taste quite foreign to you, since you're used to stale—"

"Have you ever had wine?" Hope cut in. "I find it is either something you love or hate."

Lane glanced up from the glass, to Edward's slightly quirked eyebrow, to Hope's warm expression. She wouldn't let Edward embarrass him if she could help it. He appreciated the effort.

"Only what I had in a little church in El Paso once," he told her. "I think I was about five, so I don't remember it."

She raised her glass and swirled the burgundy-colored liquid. "Wine is complex and there is a great deal of effort that goes into creating the flavor."

"Not just the flavor." Edward took a sip, swallowed, and savored it with his eyes closed. "Wine is an experience. An explosion of subtle flavors. Oak and cherry." He thought for a moment. "Hint of vanilla. Possibly a touch of cumin. Velvety. And it finishes off gently."

Lane had to force himself to keep from slapping his forehead. These two sure took their wines seriously.

Hope had a sip and considered it for a moment as well. "Oh, yes, that's lovely. A little buttery." She paused. "Yes, there's the vanilla, and possibly a touch of mushroom."

Both of them turned to Lane, expectantly. He was pondering the mushroom observation when Hope dipped her chin, nudging him.

"Well," Lane picked up his glass, "here goes." He took a tentative sip. Fought to control a grimace. He nearly burst out with, *'People enjoy this?'* But managed to cut off the comment.

"Before you say anything," Hope raised her hand in a pleading gesture, "try to think about what you tasted."

Lane focused on all the odd flavors in his mouth, but couldn't settle on anything. A little flustered, he took another sip. Since he knew what to expect, this one wasn't as jarring. After a moment, he nodded, almost amazed. "Yeah. Oak." There was a sweetness, too. "There's the grape. And vanilla." He set down the glass and nodded, but it wasn't something he'd be inclined to make a habit of. They were still staring at him. Edward's subtly raised brow was an expression of triumph. Did he think Lane was too much of a Texas hayseed to appreciate wine? Did Lane care what Edward thought? "It's a fine drink, I suppose, but I'll stick to my whiskey."

"Yes, I understand," Hope looked down at her napkin quickly. "Wine is an acquired taste."

"And not everyone will do so," Edward raised his glass to Lane and smiled. "Pity. At least you tried."

*L*ane fumbled his way through dinner, allowing Hope to point out which fork to use for the salad and so on and so forth. At least by dessert, he knew which spoon to grab, and was no stranger to coffee. The conversation of theater, literature, and politics, however, highlighted his ignorance and he didn't say much. At least watching Hope light up at the discussions of W.S. Gilbert's new play made the beating worth it. Even if, suddenly, Lane's world felt very small.

"Excuse me, gentlemen," Hope rose, and Lane and Edward followed. "I'm going to powder my nose."

She left the table and Lane poked at his chocolate mousse. He had no doubt Edward was going to take the opportunity to say what was on his mind and waited patiently. This whole dinner was a charade, a plan, aimed at making Lane look stupid. Or at least ignorant. And not worthy of Hope.

"I don't mean to be rude, old man," Edward began, "but do you seriously think you should pursue a relationship with Hope?"

Well, 'least he doesn't beat around the bush. Lane leaned back in his chair and eyed Edward with the same stare he'd give to a growling dog about to get a good, swift kick. "What I seriously think about anything is no concern of yours."

Edward huffed. "Right there is an example of my meaning. You don't care about Hope. What makes her happy. She's called to greater things. What can you offer her here, in this grubby little town?" Edward snatched his napkin from his lap and tossed it on the table. "I would bet you've never even read Shakespeare."

Lane didn't deign to answer. Just held Edward's gaze.

The man's pretty-boy face took on a hard edge and he

leaned forward a little. "You may be some sort of excellent marksman and rugged frontiersman, but let me tell you what I see. You're a low-born, uneducated, uncouth, poorly paid *cowboy*."

Cowboy. Edward said the word as if Lane was a worm. Scum floating on stagnant water. Lane's jaw tightened and his pulse ticked up. Well, if the man wanted a fight...

"And what's more, I'll make sure Hope sees you in the proper light. When she does, she'll be done with this nonsense of being a doctor in this filthy, hardscrabble town."

"And go back to Philadelphia with you? As a nurse? As your wife?"

Edward grinned, showing perfect, pearly white teeth. "Yes."

Lane had no time for a reply as Hope approached the table but didn't take her seat. "Edward, I have enjoyed our dinner. Very much actually, but I need to get home. Thank you for going to all this trouble."

Slowly, Lane rose to his feet, shadowed by Edward. "Yeah, it was one interesting meal." Lane grinned as well, though it was as fake as Edward's icy smile.

"No trouble at all." He then shifted to Hope, and his expression warmed considerably. "My dear, we'll do this again." He kissed her on the cheek. "Now that we're all friends, I'll plan more festive dinners."

"Please tell Lucy the duck was magnificent."

"I certainly will."

Lane lightly clutched Hope's arm and walked away with her, but stopped just shy of the restaurant entrance. "You know, I didn't thank Edward properly. Give me just a second."

Without waiting for Hope to reply, Lane pivoted and walked back to Edward, who was still standing at the table, watching them. Lane offered his hand and as Edward took it, said, "It is not in the stars to hold our destiny...but in ourselves. Julius Caesar, Act One, Scene Two." He winked at Edward. "Thanks for dinner, pard."

CHAPTER 3

*H*ope clung tighter to Lane as they strolled down the boardwalk. A gentle snow was falling, the flakes visible intermittently in the street lamps. Nearing eight o'clock, the avenue was empty, except for one wagon loaded with lumber rumbling along. Hope noted absently it looked to be heading to the MP&G sawmill out on the south edge of town. She was more concerned about Lane's grim expression and pronounced silence.

"I'm sorry. I know that probably wasn't the best dinner you've ever attended."

He shrugged and gave her a wry grin as they passed beneath a streetlamp. "Best company I've ever had—well, mostly."

"I don't think Edward was purposely trying to embarrass you. I simply think he doesn't know he's an obnoxious, effete snob."

They walked several feet in silence, and she didn't rush him. Finally, Lane stopped and turned to her. "You're a long way from Philadelphia, fancy wines, and the opera. Edward was doing his best tonight to make you homesick."

Hope leaned into him a little, half-smiled at the unruly springs of blond hair poking out from beneath his hat and ruffled his string tie. "If that was his best, then I suggest to you it was an exercise in futility."

"You reckon?"

Oh, he was precious. She touched his cheek. "I reckon."

Lane clutched her fingers. "Say, your hands are cold. Let's get you home."

They strode on at a more determined pace, but Hope couldn't shake the feeling Lane was more affected by Edward and his fancy dinner than he was letting on. And it worried her. If he could just understand Edward was—well, just being Edward.

At her door, Hope determined to reassure him. "He can bring every kind of wine in the world to Defiance. It won't change how I feel about the town...or you." Something flickered in Lane's eyes as he rested his hands on her hips. Regret? Insecurity? She stood on her tiptoes and kissed him. After an instant's hesitation, he returned the kiss, and Hope's pulse soared. But Lane broke the embrace too soon and stepped back from her.

"You get some rest." He tapped her on the nose, but the gesture seemed a touch listless. In spite of her thought, she flashed him a warm grin. "I'll see you tomorrow?"

He pursed his lips, thought for a moment, and then shook his head. "I've got a lot of work tomorrow. Charles is waiting on some reports from me. I don't want to promise if I can't keep my word."

Another thing Hope adored about Lane—his honor. "Well, you'll know where to find me."

*L*ane kicked at the powdery snow as he trekked back toward the livery. Never one to much care what any man thought of him, he was perturbed how Edward's insults kept playing in his mind.

You're a low-born, uneducated, uncouth, poorly paid cowboy... You don't care about Hope. She's called to greater things. What can you offer her here, in this grubby little town?

That was just it. He did care. Frustrated, Lane shoved his hands into his pockets and shrugged away a chill.

He hadn't meant to step into this quicksand. Initially, Hope had been kind of a challenge. But now he'd gone and played with fire. Let his heart rope him into a mess. And Hope was looking back at him like...like maybe her heart had roped her into the same mess.

So, what did that mean?

If she'd been anybody else, any other woman—a cook, a barkeep, heck, a schoolteacher—but she was a doctor. From Philadelphia society. She liked operas and wine.

Lane was a ranch hand. A foreman, true, but a glorified cowboy, nonetheless. And while he did have some education and a good job, he was no doctor. Like Edward.

Edward understood her world. Maybe he understood Hope.

And someone like him would certainly provide better for her. What would Lane ever offer? If he was fortunate, a big, successful ranch, sure. But it was still years away.

He sighed, disgusted with these roiling thoughts. "Lane Chandler," he muttered aloud, "you should back away from this one. You know darn well you should."

And he could—if it came down to it. Because, contrary to what Mr. Fancy-Pants Edward thought, Lane did care about Hope and what was best for her. He cared about that more than he even wanted to admit.

*H*ope had to treat all kinds of patients and she didn't mind. Considering the way the citizens of Denver had treated her, she was tickled to have any patients at all. So, even though an inkling of concern wiggled in the back of her mind, she cracked the door of her cabin to two men. The stench of filth and whiskey nearly took her breath, but she forced back her gag reflex.

One man, hugely obese and quite slovenly in his unwashed, threadbare clothing, held up a much smaller man, who slumped against his comrade, holding his right arm tightly to his chest.

After peering through the slender opening, Hope peeled the door back a little further. "Yes, gentlemen, what can I do for you?"

"My friend here needs a doctor, ma'am," the fat one said.

Hope assessed the pair, but knew she couldn't turn them away. "All right. Go to my office. I'll be there directly."

In the pre-dawn darkness, she changed quickly, swiped up the key to the office and raced over through more falling snow.

*T*he smaller man, it turned out, had nothing more than a dislocated shoulder. Painful, excruciatingly tender to the touch—judging by his yowls of pain—but relatively easy to fix. With a good, swift snatch, and a braying screech from the man, Hope had him restored in an instant. She was surprised, as inebriated as he was, he felt a thing.

Sitting on her examination table, he rotated his arm, teetering with the movement, and then he grinned. "Yeah, that feels much better, Doc. Thanks. Let's have a drink to celebrate!"

"No, I couldn't. Today is not a holiday for me. But thank you for the offer."

"Aw, come on," the fat man said, rising from his seat at the window. "Let's have a snort." He produced a bottle of whiskey from his coat pocket and waved it in the air.

"Gentlemen, again, I appreciate the offer, but no thank you. If you'll kindly pay me, I need to get ready for the day. There are probably other revelers—"

"You ain't being very friendly," the fat man said, a scowl darkening his chubby face. "She ain't being very friendly, Len."

Len slid off the examination table and again rotated his arm. "Oh, yeah, I might live now. You got to have a drink with us, Doc, to celebrate."

Both men moved toward Hope and she took a step back. How had relocating a shoulder turned into this? And Edward wasn't due for another hour. "I'm asking you to leave," she said firmly, forcing fear from her voice. "Surely you can understand as the town doctor I do not need to imbibe."

"Doc Cook had a snort with us now and then."

"I'm not Doc—Doctor Cook."

The two men exchanged leering grins and then suddenly Len grabbed Hope. She couldn't believe their intent and she wasn't going to accept it lightly. Kicking, screaming, squealing, fighting, she gave him a run for his money, but the other man stepped in and before Hope could do much more, her arms were snugged behind her. She was pulled tightly against the fat man's chest and now Len had the bottle of whiskey. Immobilized, fear clutched Hope's heart.

He raised it near her face and caressed a strand of her hair that had fallen free in the struggle. "You can take a drink, or I'll give you a drink."

Hope thought about screaming for help but no one was close enough to hear. She had to get away, run for the sheriff. She struggled again, kicking the fat man in the knee. He yowled in her ear and Len immediately stepped in and grabbed Hope's face.

"Here ya go, little sister."

He poured the liquor and Hope writhed, twisted, pulled away from him. The whiskey splashed over her face, down her chin, and onto her dress—

A loud banging at the front door brought the horseplay to a standstill as the men swung to face the noise. Hope thought she might faint with relief. Lane stood in the doorway, a saddle lying on the floor at his feet, his gun drawn and pointing at Hope's attackers.

"I don't know what's going on here, but it's over now. Cowell, let her go before I put a bullet square in the center of your forehead."

Cowell released Hope as if she'd suddenly turned into a writhing snake, pushed her away, and raised his hands, as did Len. Sobbing with relief, Hope rushed to Lane, nearly tripping over the saddle. Falling into his outstretched arm, weeping and hiccuping, she wiped the vile liquid off her face and her dress. They could have done anything to her. They could have—

"Shhh. It's all right now," he said softly. "You're all right now."

Hope scolded herself mentally for her cowardice, sniffed and straightened up. But they had terrified her. Overpowered her completely. "I'm sorry." She fought with herculean effort to hold back any more sobs. No more. She couldn't cry anymore in front of these men.

"Nothing to be sorry for. I'd cry, too, if Cowell hugged me. If his smell didn't kill me first."

Cowell's face darkened and his lip lifted in a sneer. "You

ain't funny, Lane. Not at all. And we wasn't gonna hurt the little lady. She shouldn't have been so uppity."

Lane glared at Len like he wanted to rip off the sot's head. "Was that gonna make you feel better, Len? Huh? You feel like a big man, pouring liquor down a woman's throat? I oughta beat the hound out of you both."

"Put that Colt away," Cowell motioned toward Lane's holster, "and give it a go."

Lane took a long, deep breath, calming himself, Hope believed. "Boy, wouldn't I like to. And, while that would make me feel some better, Cowell, right now I'm gonna enjoy watching you spend a few days in jail, and using your own money to post bail..." Lane's voice picked up an ominous edge, "then maybe we'll try it your way." He patted Hope's shoulder. "You all right? I doubt they would have hurt you. They ain't known for violence, just shenanigans."

"I'm fine, I'm fine." She wiped her eyes but couldn't seem to find the strength to let go of Lane. "I'll be fine." The quiver in her voice humiliated her. Why couldn't she steady herself?

"I need to escort these two over to see Beckwith." He dropped his arm.

At first, Hope didn't comprehend, but Lane subtly shrugged his shoulder. "Oh, yes, of course." Hope stepped back, wiping her eyes and glaring at Len and Cowell. She wasn't so sure about their intentions. Not at all. Regardless, to be so helpless, so overpowered, was demoralizing in a way she'd never experienced.

"By the way, the saddle. It's your Christmas present, Hope."

Hope glanced down. It was a lovely tan saddle covered in intricate tooling. She grabbed the pommel and dragged it out of the way. "It's lovely." She started laughing. "In fact, it's the most beautiful thing I've ever seen. Thank you." He'd even tied a big, fat, albeit rough, red bow around the horn.

Thank you, God, for this saddle and the timing of its delivery.

Lane chuckled. "Funny. You weren't supposed to be here. I was gonna leave it on the porch as a hint." He shook his head, apparently marveling over the way things had worked out. "Well, come on you two. I've got a busy day ahead." He checked with Hope one last time. "You're sure you're all right?"

She managed a slight nod and a weak smile. She had to be all right. Cowell and Len, scowling viciously at Lane, their hands still raised, shuffled toward the door.

"I'll be back, to check on—"

Suddenly, Len lobbed the nearly empty bottle of liquor at Lane with powerful force. Reflexively, Lane used the hand holding the gun to block it and the revolver went flying. Cowell was sober enough to see the opportunity and, growling like a drunken bear, lunged for Lane. Hope screamed.

---

*C*oiled together like snakes, Cowell and Lane hurtled over Hope's desk, crashing to the floor in a barrage of bone-crunching blows. Hope stood frozen in terror. She couldn't grasp how to help or stop this—

The gun, a voiceless whisper said. At that instant, she looked at Len and he looked back at her as if he'd heard the same thought. Lane and Cowell rose to their feet. The thud of fists on flesh was accompanied by grunts and gasps. Len and Hope's gazes shot to the Colt lying on the floor near the back wall. They both seemed to ponder the chances of grabbing it. They moved then, simultaneously. He lunged for it, as did Hope, but he was closer. A medical vapor lamp, made of stout iron, sat on the counter. As Len came up, swinging the gun, Hope swung the lamp with everything in her, catching the man in the temple. He collapsed and dropped the gun as suddenly as if he'd sniffed chloroform.

Behind her, she heard the sound of another body hitting the floor and spun, raising the lamp in case Cowell was still standing. To her amazement, Edward had a white cloth in his hand, was pressing it to Cowell's face, and slowly laying the drunk on the floor.

In an instant, the man was sprawled out, dead to the world. Lane was on his feet—barely—swaying, huffing and puffing, and bleeding from his mouth and fists. His hair was a disheveled mess. Edward, rising to his feet, frowned as if he found Lane's appearance unacceptable. Sniffing, he walked the cloth over to the sink and that was when Hope saw the open bottle of chloroform in his hand.

"Would someone like to tell me what has transpired here?" he said, putting the cloth and bottle in the sink. "We'll need to find the cork for that," he muttered absently, turning to them.

Hope quickly scanned the mess she called her office. Her desk had been knocked on its side, the two guest chairs lay shattered in a million pieces on the floor, the curtain separating the waiting room from the examination room was hanging by a thread—literally. Her framed diplomas lay on the floor in piles of glass and wood.

But Lane was still standing. She rushed over to him and helped him make his way to the examination table. He leaned on it, breathing like a winded mule. "Drunk or sober, Cowell packs a wallop." He worked his jaw back and forth and flinched.

"Let me get you cleaned up." She immediately went about gathering cotton balls, bandages, and alcohol.

"Really, Mr. Chandler, was this necessary?" Edward kicked at a splintered piece of the ladder back chair.

Lane touched a puffy, upper lip and grimaced. "Sorry I

wasn't more thoughtful of your furniture as I was protecting Hope."

Edward inclined his head as she began cleaning Lane's face. "What exactly happened here?"

"The one man had a dislocated shoulder. After I straightened him out, they proceeded to try to force a drink on me. Lane changed their minds."

Scowling, Edward squatted down at Len's side, checked the man's pulse at his wrist, then dropped the limp hand like a piece of trash. "Out cold." He stood, heaving a great sigh as if all this was more of an annoyance than he could bear. "Did you have to do it with so much..." he looked around the destroyed room, "vulgar force?"

Hope saw the sneer try to rear up on Lane's mouth, but he held it down and met her gaze. "My apologies. I didn't know where you kept the chloroform."

"Thank you," she whispered, dabbing at his mouth. "I'm sorry I was such a—"

Lane laid his fingers to her lips. "They're a rough pair. Though not normally taken to scaring women. 'Course, after the way you swung that vapor lamp, they should be scared of you."

She smiled at him. "Thank you so much for the saddle."

"A horse comes with it, too. Soon as I find the right one. You gonna live out here, you've got to learn to ride."

CHAPTER 4

*H*ope was pretty shaken, and Lane didn't like seeing her that way. Drumming his fingers on his thigh, he leaned back on the wall at Sheriff Beckwith's office and watched the marshal lock up the two miscreants. A gun in their backs, they'd been perfect gentlemen on the way here, but Lane suspected some damage had been done to Hope—a chip in her resolve to love and serve Defiance. Edward would capitalize on it, too.

"I'll set the bond high," Beckwith grumbled, taking a seat at his desk. The flinty old lawman was obviously pretty annoyed. With sharp, angry movements, he snatched a journal over in front of him and flipped it open to a blank page. "Going after the town doctor like that." He swiped up a pencil and started writing. "You should have laid them both out, Lane."

"I thought hard about it, trust me." He touched his lip, tender and slightly swollen. "But I didn't think Hope should see it." He pushed off the wall and strode over to the cell holding the two offenders. "Come here." They rose from their cots and shuffled to the bars. Lane stared hard at them for a minute, until they dropped their gazes and shifted uncomfortably. "In a few days," he said, "I want you both to shave, bathe, put on some clean clothes and make yourselves presentable."

Len rubbed his jaw, suspicion glinting in his dark eyes. "What for?"

"You're gonna march yourselves over to Dr. Clark's office —at a decent hour—and apologize to her. Show her you can act like you've got some manners. Apologize to her and make her believe you wouldn't have hurt her."

Both men huffed, grumbled, but Cowell shook his head. "I'm done with the lady doctor. I don't want to see her again for nothing."

Lane leaned in and held the man's gaze. "You don't go apologize to her in a manner befittin' a gentleman, I promise you—you will have *need* of a doctor."

It only took an instant for the threat to sink in. Cowell and Len cleared their throats and moved back a hair from the bars, Len rubbing the goose egg on his head. Lane raised his eyebrows, waiting for a clear answer.

Len nodded.

After a moment, Cowell did as well.

*A*s Edward rehung the curtain, and Hannah Page, the young nurse-in-training, took splintered chair parts out to the burn pile, Hope finished putting her desk back in order. For two hours now Edward had been hammering away at what a vulgar, violent place this Defiance was. A physician wasn't safe in his own office—especially a female physician.

Yes, he was reveling in the disaster. No, he hadn't said it openly, but Hope could see it in his eyes. Even if a woman doctor had patients, she wasn't safe to live in a place like this alone. And Hope couldn't help but wonder if she *was* cut out for this life. Those two men had scared the wits out of her. They had frightened her more than getting stabbed. That night, she couldn't see the attacker. And it had happened so quickly.

This morning, Cowell and Len, they had grabbed her, overpowered her, forced the liquor on her. They had not only scared her, they'd degraded her, made her feel...truly helpless.

Oh, Lord, please tell me Defiance is done dishing out this violence...

"That is a lovely saddle," Hannah said, coming in the back and spying it by the door. The girl, only seventeen, had started training as a nurse under the previous physician in Defiance. She'd proven to be invaluable to Hope, both with assistance and counsel. "And Lane's right, you do need to learn to ride. You might not always be able to go off in a buggy."

Suddenly exhausted, Hope sat down at her desk. "Ride? Learn to ride? I'm beginning to think I need to learn to shoot."

"Not a bad skill to have," Hannah said nonchalantly, grabbing the broom and sweeping up some glass they'd missed.

Hope was nonplused by the girl's acquiescence to the idea. Maybe Hope didn't want to learn to shoot. Maybe she didn't want to live in a place where that was considered as handy as knowing how to ride a horse.

Maybe she wasn't the pioneer she thought she was, after all. She doubted pioneer women fell apart at being accosted by ruffians. On the verge of more tears, and despising them, Hope abruptly excused herself.

*L*ane didn't know what to make of Hannah's news. Hope had just jumped up and run out of the office, the girl had said. It worried Hannah. It worried him.

Shed of his prisoners, he was returning to check on Hope again at the office when he'd run into Hannah in the yard. She was on her way to Hope's cottage, assuming the good doctor had escaped there. Lane had convinced Hannah to let him make the house call.

Now, his hand poised to knock on the door, he wasn't sure this was a wise idea, after all. He'd never been much good at comforting females. Before he could turn tail and run, Hope slowly opened the door and greeted him with a shaky smile. Her eyes, blue as the Colorado sky in September, were rimmed in red and the tip of her nose was pink.

She sniffed and moistened her lips. "I'm all right if that's why you're here."

"Hannah did say you skedaddled out of the office all of a sudden."

Hope sighed heavily and turned away from him. He took it as an invitation and stepped in, shutting the door behind him. Hope ambled over to the pot-bellied stove and just stood there, staring down at it. *At least she isn't crying,* Lane thought with relief. *Still, she ain't herself, either.*

"Hope, um, you upset about what happened this morning?"

She hugged herself and sort of waggled her head. "I am upset over..." her voice came out choked, "several things really, but those two horrible men put things in perspective."

"Those two can't put a thought together, much less anything into perspective."

Hope grunted and rounded on him slowly. "They can't, but I can. I can't stop thinking about the *what-ifs.* What if they'd intended more harm? What if you hadn't shown up? What if Edward had shown up and walked in on those ruffians? What if—"

"Stop it." Lane double-timed it over to her and clutched her shoulders. "What-ifs'll drive you crazy." He had his own experience with them, for sure. "You can't let your mind go there. Everything turned out all right."

A scowl covered her pretty little face and she snatched free of him. "I'm no frontier doctor. I'm a woman playing at being a doctor. Edward's right—this is no place for a tinhorn like me."

"You dropped that label a long time ago. When you saved Ledford from choking right there in the middle of the restaurant. Did surgery on Two Spears and now he's still got the use of his arm. Heck, you've even been stabbed and shook it off—"

"I didn't shake it off." She snapped back, her tone crackling with hysteria. "I pushed it to the back of my mind. I was convinced nothing like that would happen—" Her voice broke and she took a step back as if moving away from a wild animal. Her chin quivered and her eyes filled with tears. "…Would happen again."

Instinctively, Lane crushed her into a tight hug and held on to her. She fought him for a moment, but eventually gave up and melted against him. He could feel her tears wetting his shirt. He stroked her head and whispered, "Shh. Shh." He kissed the top of her head. "You've had a fright. Just give yourself time. You're tough. You'll be all right."

"No." She shook her head back and forth, but didn't look up at him. "No. I don't belong here. A town like Defiance needs a male doctor."

"*L*ane, I am beyond shocked at you."

Embarrassment heating his face, Lane tugged at his collar as Charles leaned back in his fancy, leather chair. He stared at Lane, his usually supremely confident expression now painted with amazement. He tilted his head and traced his jet black mustache thoughtfully. "In all the years I have known you, I've never once heard you express doubts about being a cowboy."

"You misunderstand. It ain't my job I'm doubting. I'm just doubting my association with Dr. Clark."

"Because she's a doctor?"

"Because I'm not sure she's gonna stay."

McIntyre's eyes lit with curiosity or amusement—Lane wasn't sure—and one eyebrow quirked up. "You want her to stay?"

"Well, I don't see much point in courtin' a woman who's gonna be on the next stage out of here. And much as I hate to admit it, Edward made some good points the other night. Cowell and Len showing her their best side sure didn't help."

"Personally, I don't think you're giving Dr. Clark enough credit, or yourself. If Edward could ride one mile in your saddle, he'd tip his hat and head back East." Charles tapped his index finger on his blotter. "But *she* has grit. This world will suit her, you watch."

"I don't know. She seems pretty rattled right now."

"You're suited to this life, Lane. Show her she is, too. No matter what she's faced."

"You didn't hear her, Charles. The shine has worn off Defiance for her, I'm afraid."

Charles raised his chin, studied Lane intently for a moment. "Make up your mind. Fight for her or not. But be sure," he raised his index finger and pointed it at Lane, "you are fighting for the right reasons. Don't dally with the good doctor. Naomi will have your head."

"I ain't dallying with her."

"Then you're in love."

"I—" Lane stopped, unsure what he was about to say. A denial didn't feel right. But he wasn't dallying with Hope. Sooo, the alternative…

His confusion melted into anger and he surged to his feet. "I have to go check on a fence crew." He snatched his hat off Charles' desk and stormed from the boss's office, furious over the chuckling that followed after him.

his world will suit her, you watch.

Lane tugged into his gloves and stepped out on to Charles' porch. He glanced over at the cowboys moving a remuda of horses out across the snow-covered hills, headed to the fenced acreage down the valley. A hundred acres gave the animals room to run and it wasn't far from the barn, which made taking hay out easier.

He shifted his gaze off to the west. A quarter-mile away, the new barn, the one built when they'd tried keeping healthy cattle separate from the plague-infected animals, was stacked to the rafters with Timothy and alfalfa. Plenty of feed for the horses and the small herd of Angus and Herefords he'd brought up from Gunnison. Lane was intent on making sure all the King M livestock was fat and sassy for spring.

Managing the range and the feed, counting and watching over the calves and foals that would be born, keeping the ranch maintained and the men on task, procuring a new herd from Texas—it all added up to a lot of work. None of it easy. And, no, he didn't go to school to learn to do it. Ranching came naturally to him and he liked it. A lot.

Dang, he wouldn't trade a second of it for any rare bottle of wine or even front row tickets to see Lily Langtree. And while he didn't want to give a rip about what Edward thought, some of his ideas might be…intriguing to Hope.

On the other hand, Lane believed he could convince Hope of the beauty in a rugged, small-town life. It would challenge her, and she would add some high-quality doctoring to the area. She could make a real difference out here. A lot to be said for that. Best of all, he could give Hope one thing Edward couldn't: freedom. Lane wanted Hope to practice medicine as a doctor.

However, the question remained, was he dallying with the woman?

Or was he in love with Hope?

Lane decided he just wouldn't worry about that question right now. He'd get his mind back on something he knew a little more about.

Nodding to himself, he stepped off the porch.

CHAPTER 5

*H*ope drummed her fingers on the desk and stared out at the falling snow. Snow kept the office slow. Ailments were less urgent when one had to trudge through a foot of it to seek medical attention. And what if someone needed a house call? She could drive a wagon. As could Edward and Hannah, but if the snow got any deeper, a single horse would be more serviceable. As would snowshoes. Neither of the two prospects appealed to her.

"The break will do you good," Hannah said, folding a bandage. She added it to the stack beside her on the counter and turned to face Hope. "Besides, it's Christmas Eve."

With a sigh, Hope rose and ambled over to her young nurse. Hope suspected the girl's inquisitive blue eyes, long golden braid, and angelic features drew as many fakers as sick men in for medical attention. "And tomorrow is Christmas. You should have the day off to spend with your husband and son."

The tilt to Hannah's head and the lifting of her brow said she had her mind set. "You've got to take some time for yourself. Besides," Hannah rolled her eyes toward Examination Room One, its door closed. "Dr. Pratt will be here the whole day, while my boys and I slip out to the ranch for Christmas dinner."

Hope tucked a stray auburn strand loosely back into her bun. She was looking forward to spending the night at the McIntyre's ranch. She was eager to see their home, but especially to spend time with Lane. He'd promised to take her riding and show her some surprises. "All right. But I may ride back in with you, if that's all right. Save Lane the trip."

"If you're sure." Hannah glanced at the closed door as she worried her bottom lip. "Does Dr. Pratt have any plans? I feel a little sorry for him being alone on Christmas."

Hope smiled. Few people in town had warmed up to the pompous know-it-all who used to be Hope's fiancé, but at least Hannah was kind enough to concern herself with his welfare. "He asked if he could drop by my place for some eggnog." She shrugged and lowered her voice. "I said yes because I felt sorry for him."

Hannah frowned. "What about Lane?"

"What about him?"

"You don't think it will bother him, you having a male guest on Christmas night?"

Hope picked up a bandage and refolded it. "I haven't told him. I wasn't sure it was—I mean, I haven't decided if he should know." She set the cloth down and huffed. "I suppose I should tell him, at least mention it, but Lane and I have no formal understanding. Besides, Edward is merely an old friend now. There's nothing romantic between us."

Hannah's eyes narrowed down to slits. "If you're hiding it from Lane, it's wrong."

"I'm not hiding it." Hope folded her arms, expressing her unhappiness over this situation. "It's just that Edward is here alone, and I also feel sorry for him. I'm not sure Lane would understand, and I'm not sure he even has a right to an opinion about the matter."

Hannah sagged as if she was disappointed in Hope. "Well, sounds like you two should get that ironed out."

"And how do you propose I do that?"

"Start by telling Lane you'll be with him Christmas Day and Dr. Pratt Christmas night."

Hope flinched. "That makes me sound like a flirt."

Hannah raised her eyebrows but didn't speak the accusation.

"I'm not a flirt. I just don't know what I want, exactly. I don't know if I'm staying here. I don't know if I'm cut out for this life. I don't know what Lane wants."

"What do you think Dr. Pratt wants?"

"Now? I suppose he'd dance with glee if he knew I was thinking seriously about heading back to Philadelphia. Therefore, I won't tell him. I think he's given up on trying to force the issue."

"You believe that?"

"Yes, why shouldn't I?"

Hannah glanced again at the closed door. "I think he's just given up the frontal assault."

"And I think you're mistaken." Hope returned to her desk and sat down to finish writing her patient notes.

---

*H*ope set her valise on the bed and looked around the guest room. A small, river rock fireplace warmed the homey atmosphere of log walls, Indian rugs, and large brass bed—the fanciest piece of furniture in the room.

"It's probably a little rustic for someone like you—"

"Nonsense." Hope pivoted to her hostess, Naomi McIntyre. Hannah's sister, the woman was similar in appearance—long, blonde hair, petite bone structure, delicate features—but at least a decade older. And very close to having a baby. Her abdomen protruded proudly. *Less than a month*, Hope thought absently. "The room is lovely and I'm so appreciative of your invitation. I've never spent Christmas on a ranch."

"And I know Lane is eager to show it to you."

"Naomi, do you ever get bored here?" Hope was surprised the question unexpectedly leaped forth, but Naomi seemed so contented, or so Hope thought after every doctor visit. "Do you miss your home back in….?"

"North Carolina? I miss a few things about it. Winter is easier there, certainly, but no. Defiance, this valley, our ranch—I'm home." Naomi inclined her head, golden strands of hair cascading down her shoulder. "Are you bored? Please say Defiance isn't wearing you out already?"

"Bored? No, no. Quite the opposite." *Quite…* "I guess I find myself wondering…"

"About Lane?"

Hope nodded, deciding not to voice her doubts about her pioneer spirit or Lane's intentions in the relationship.

"Well, I think he might be doing a little wondering, too. Eventually, you'll both figure it out."

"You see him more than Hannah. He is larger than life, full of confidence, and so indomitable. Nothing seems to frighten him. Is he—do you think he could be—serious about me…?" If he was, would it impact Hope's plan to leave? And, oh, how she dreaded sharing that information with Naomi.

Naomi folded her arms and rested them on her abdomen, smiling. "The cowboys call it swagger. Lane has a lot of swagger. And often it just whitewashes a man's desire to hunt and capture."

"Seize the treasure, as it were?"

"Yes."

"And you think that's what Lane is doing with me? Merely lining up a conquest?"

"No." Naomi took a deep breath, let it out slowly, as if choosing her words carefully. "I think Lane is in unfamiliar territory." Hope waited, expecting more, but Naomi shook her head. "I can't see the future, Hope. Pray and ask God to show you two what he wants for you. And then listen."

"Lane told me once he wasn't all that religious. At least not as religious as his mother."

"Could be God will use you to draw Lane closer to Him." Naomi laid a hand on Hope's arm. "Put God first, no matter what happens. Then you'll have the strength and confidence to handle the outcome."

---

*H*ope was stunned to learn the table spread with an amazing array of food on Christmas Eve wouldn't hold a candle to what was planned for Christmas Day. Tonight, a ham sat in the middle, surrounded by candied yams, cranberries, mashed potatoes, and a smorgasbord of pies, cakes, and cookies.

"And there will be more tomorrow?" She asked in amazement as Naomi and their cook Maria set down two more pies.

"Oh, yes," Naomi said, laughing. "Tomorrow the ranch hands will come in and eat with us. Tonight, it's just you and Lane, Ian and Rebecca, Charles, Two Spears and me."

Again, a pang of guilt smarted in Hope's heart. "I'm sorry Hannah isn't here tonight."

Naomi waved away her complaint. "She was more than

delighted to have a quiet Christmas Eve with her own family. She's certainly waited long enough for it—"

Stomping and muffled conversation interrupted her and drew their attention to the front door. Mr. McIntyre and Lane let themselves in, along with a swirl of snow. The ladies rushed to greet them and help them slip out of their cold coats and hats.

Mr. McIntyre let Naomi pull the woolen coat from him and then turned and gave his bride a quick kiss. "Merry Christmas Eve, Your Ladyship."

"Merry Christmas Eve, husband."

Lane offered Hope an embarrassed grin as the kiss between husband and wife created an awkwardness—and possibly ideas—in both of them. Hope cleared her throat and took Lane's coat. "Snowing, is it?" She asked, hanging his coat on the rack next to the door.

"Only flurries," Lane answered, peeling out of his gloves.

"Enough to make it slippery for the rodeo tomorrow." Mr. McIntyre shook the melted snow from his dark locks.

"Rodeo?" Hope asked.

"Tradition." Lane took her by the elbow and the two couples strode to the long, bountiful table. Appreciative whistles accompanied *oohs* and *aahs* from the hungry men. "You and Maria have outdone yourselves, Miss Naomi." Lane patted his stomach. "That is a meal fit for a king."

"Thank you. Why don't we sit and have some coffee while we wait for Ian and Rebecca? I'm sure you two could use it."

"Amen to that," Mr. McIntyre said, pulling out a chair for his wife.

Lane did the same for Hope and then settled beside her. She touched his hand lightly. "You were telling me about a rodeo."

"Oh, yeah. Every year. We have Christmas dinner then go find out who's the best roper and rider."

"It's been a toss-up between Lane and Emilio," Mr. McIntyre said, sipping on his coffee.

Naomi's eyes darted to four chairs still vacant. "We had half-way hoped Emilio and Mollie would be back from Kansas, but they're staying through Christmas."

Emilio, the young Hispanic boy who worked on the ranch, and Mollie, formerly one of Mr. McIntyre's soiled doves, had found new lives and new eyes for each other. "I hope they come back," Hope said. "I like them both."

"I miss them terribly," Naomi lifted her cup for Maria to fill.

"I know the ranch sure feels Emilio's absence," Lane said, offering his cup to the rotund, little Mexican woman. "Gracias."

"No, thank you." Mr. McIntyre waved her away from refilling his cup. "It'll be a test, for both of them. Emilio loves Mollie, but he loves this ranch and his family here. He told me that before he left. I told him to take his time and be sure of his next move."

Naomi reached over and squeezed his hand. "I think he'll come back. Mollie—I don't know. She missed her mother something fierce." She shook her head as if clearing away sad thoughts and grinned at Lane. "I doubt he'll be able to stay away from his best friend."

"Yeah, I am prettier than Mollie anyway."

"True," Naomi said, nodding. "Emilio was telling me exactly that just before they left for Kansas." The group chuckled over the nonsense.

"My mother's favorite holiday was Christmas." Hope was lost in the memory of the scent of cinnamon in the air, shimmering glass bulbs on a tree, and her mother's rich, clear laughter ringing in the parlor. Momentarily, she realized everyone was staring. "My mother passed away when I was ten."

"I'm sorry," Naomi said.

"No, it's all right. It's been a long time. I don't remember her very well anymore. But I do remember how Christmas seemed to last forever. She decorated everywhere. Baked every day. Went about the house singing carols. I wish I was more like her. Here it is Christmas Eve and I didn't put up the first decoration."

"There's always next year," Lane said, sipping on his mug.

"Lord willing," Naomi added.

"Lord willing," Mr. McIntyre repeated, his gaze drifting off as well. "Quite the year, this last one. I am sure next year will be better."

Naomi patted her stomach. "It will be. We'll be starting off with a new member of our family."

He grinned like a fool and patted her hand. "Children. I never thought anything would terrify me so. I don't think having a noose around my neck was as frightening as the prospect of fouling up a child."

Naomi shuddered. "Oh, please, let's not revisit that ordeal. I'll take child-rearing any day."

In an apparent effort to lighten the mood, he nodded across the table at Lane. "I told Naomi if it's a boy we're naming him Lane—"

"And if it's a girl," Naomi interrupted, "we're naming her Lane."

Laughter erupted around the table and Lane actually blushed. "Aw, heck…"

"We're honored to name our baby after you, Lane." Naomi took a deep breath as if holding back tears. "Honored."

"There's gotta be better choices. Poor kid'll have to carry the moniker forever."

Hope smiled at his embarrassment. "A rose by any other name—"

42

HEATHER BLANTON

"Would still smell as sweet," Mr. McIntyre finished.

More laughter, but she noted Lane's faded first. Was he at all familiar with Shakespeare?

"Romeo and Juliet," Naomi said wistfully. "My, there's a story."

"Oh, I know," Hope clutched her heart. Her favorite Shakespeare tale of all. But probably dismally boring to a man like Lane. She reigned in her enthusiasm. "But I sometimes think the Bard is much ado about—well, not *nothing*, but…"

"I have on occasion, thought" Mr. McIntyre agreed, "yes, some of his work is a bit maudlin."

"Lane," Hope turned to him, determined not to make him suffer through another high-brow conversation, "what do you like to read?"

Mr. McIntyre snorted. "Stock reports and ranching quarterlies."

Lane scowled playfully at his friend. "I pick up a Sears catalog every now and then, too."

Before anyone could offer more saucy returns, Ian and Rebecca knocked as they entered, snow again making its way into the entrance. Naomi and Mr. McIntyre rose to welcome them. Shivering and shrugging out of his coat to Naomi's waiting hands, Ian smiled warmly at his sister-in-law. "I hope ye've room for houseguests. I dinnae see us driving back to town in this weather."

"Lane!" Two Spears' shrill voice from outside brought Lane instantly to his feet. The young Indian boy burst into the house, his dark eyes frantically searching the room. "Lane, Dolly is foaling!"

"Dang," Lane whispered. He met Hope's gaze as she rose to stand beside him. "I have to tend to this. I'm sorry."

She touched his arm, stopping him. "I'm a doctor, maybe I can help."

43

"Dolly's a horse."

"Still, I might be able to assist you."

His brow ticked up almost imperceptibly at her offer and he nodded. "Come along then."

CHAPTER 6

*T*his wasn't gonna be pretty, but Lane didn't have any choice. Dolly was on the ground, breathing hard, in full labor, but in distress. He'd seen enough foals born to have a good idea of the problem. Lane peeled out of his coat, his vest, his button-up, down to his long johns shirt. He hiked the sleeve up as high as he could, knowing full well it wouldn't be high enough. "Hope, if you'll take that feed sack and put it over her head, I'm gonna check things out."

Without hesitating, Hope pulled the burlap bag off the stall's low wall and gently placed it over Dolly's head. Lane dropped to his knees at the other end of the horse, touched her haunch gently and spoke soothingly to her for a moment. "It's all right, girl," he said, stroking her fur. "It's all right. Let me see if I can help you."

A contraction hit the animal and every muscle in her body reacted, tightening like steel bands. Lane waited for it to pass, then slowly, tenderly, inserted his arm into the birth canal. Deeper, deeper he pushed through the mass of hot, slimy, ridged muscles until he felt the foal. He closed his eyes and tried to let his fingers show him what was wrong. After a minute he had it figured out. "She's upside down and one leg is bent back," he whispered to Hope.

"Can you right her?"

"Gonna try. Keep her as calm as you can."

"Wait, I think she's having another contraction."

Lane withdrew his arm and waited for the spasm to pass. Ideally, he didn't want a limb in there during a contraction—they were downright painful. Dolly grunted, her legs shot out straight and rigid, her body tensed and strained. After a few minutes, the spasm eased off and Lane once again inserted his arm.

"All right, little buddy, let's get you situated."

"Lord," Hope prayed, "um, please guide Lane's hands."

She sounded unsure, but Lane knew she was a new Believer and he appreciated her effort all the more.

"Help him, Father, please," she continued. "Bless the skill of his hands, grant him wisdom and strength, and we thank You for the healthy life that is about to be born. In Jesus' name we pray."

"Amen," he whispered.

Lane did the best he could twisting, pulling, tugging that bent leg, working his fingers into the foal, but the sack made it difficult to get a firm grip. Finally, he felt it stretch out. "Okay, the leg's straight." Now the hard part. "I've only done this one other time." He looked at her. "I couldn't get the foal to rotate."

She nodded, understanding what was at stake. "You will this time."

"I think I'll for sure be needing that divine intervention." He took a deep breath, thought about the prayer. *Lord, I hate to lose them both and I'm liable to if this little fella doesn't roll. I would appreciate Your help...*

Lane reached deeper than he had before, splayed his fingers open and pressed on the withers, pushing the small animal. The foal jerked in protest but didn't roll. Lane tried again, slipping his hand all the way beneath him and lifted. His muscles burned from the effort, but he kept on trying. "Come on, come on…" Just one quick roll—

"Contraction coming."

He couldn't let go. He flinched as the painful vice grip of muscles clamped down on his arm, immobilizing it. At least he had the use of his hand and kept pressing, pushing, but he held his breath against the pain. The contraction eased off and suddenly the little foal rolled. "Oh, yeah, I think…" he faded off, checking to make sure. Everything felt normal now. "Hallelujah, that was it." He pulled his arm free, still throbbing from the squeeze it had been in, and fell back against the stall wall, exhausted. "All right, Dolly. It's up to you now."

Hope stepped away, bringing the burlap bag with her. "You did it."

"You did it."

Hope spun at Naomi's voice.

"Here, thought you'd be needing these." Naomi opened the stall door and handed Hope a stack of towels.

"Oh, yes, I'm sure Lane would like to clean up."

He glanced down at his right side. His arm shimmered with blood and bodily fluids. Half his shirt was soaked. And his teeth had begun to chatter. "Yes, Lane would."

Charles was behind Naomi and entered the stall carrying a buffalo robe. "Everything under control?"

"I'm no vet, but I think so."

Charles hooked his thumb in his vest pockets and studied Dolly. "You want me to send Corky or anybody to relieve you?"

"Nah." Lane climbed wearily to his feet, took a towel from Hope, but paused for an instant to share a look with her. "I think we'll be fine. If Hope gets cold, I'll send her in."

*W*hen Mr. McIntyre and Naomi left, Hope bent down and stroked Dolly's cheek. "Shhh. It's going to be all right. You're going to deliver a fine filly or colt."

She looked up to ask Lane's opinion and had to bite back a pleasantly surprised smile. He had turned his back to her and was peeling out of his nasty shirt. Lean muscles rippled down his back, across his broad shoulders, glistening, inviting her touch as he stripped. She swallowed and turned back to the horse as he reached for his button-up.

Dressed, he turned to her and extended his clean hand. "Can I have another towel?" She dutifully rose and handed him one, which he dipped in the water bucket and renewed his effort to clean his forearm, hand, and especially his fingernails.

"That was quite masterful, Lane. Skilled. You could be a veterinarian." She hugged the last remaining towel to her chest and watched him.

"That might be a tad strong." He finished, tossed the towel into the corner with the first one, slipped into his coat, then reached for the buffalo robe. He held it up and offered a sideways grin. "Care to sit under a buffalo skin with me, Dr. Clark?"

She tugged on her coat collar. "It is quite chilly in here."

In a moment, they were settled in a corner across from Dolly, watching nature unfold. A chill shot through Hope and she hugged Lane's arm. Soon warmth enveloped them both and she felt a contentment she'd never experienced. Dolly stiffened and grunted with another contraction. They were coming faster now. "Have you delivered many foals?"

"A few. I've got more experience with calves, but there don't seem to be a lot of difference."

"Have you always been a cowboy?"

He shook his head. "Not always, but mostly. For a few years right after the war, I was a Texas Ranger."

"Really? I've heard of them. Supposed to be quite tough."

"Tough?" He nodded. "Tall tales didn't match up to *them*. Tougher lot of men I've never known."

"Why did you leave? If I may ask."

"After the war, Texas wasn't too organized. The Rangers had trouble getting funded by the legislature. Sometimes the politicians used us as pawns. There was infighting, power struggles. Just wasn't for me. I like a simple life."

His face darkened as if the statement troubled him. He shifted and turned more fully to her. She couldn't help but take in his hazel eyes, warm, inviting. They searched her own, the light from the weak overhead lantern adding magic to the moment. When he didn't speak right away, she said, "What?"

"The simple life. There's a lot of things to recommend it."

"I don't disagree."

"I've read some Shakespeare. Even speak a little Latin."

"You do?"

"My ma was an educated woman. She taught us some things."

"Your mother must have been something."

"Hell on Wheels, Pa used to call her."

Hope chuckled, but Lane didn't. He was still looking at her intently as if her response to everything he was saying mattered a great deal.

"I've been to an Opera House. Saw that Italian star Adelina Patti perform in *Rigoletto*. It was all right. Interesting and everything, but you remember the Creator's Fire I showed you on the mountain that day?"

"Of course. It was beautiful." A setting sun had set a forest of aspens aglow with false but stunning fire.

"That's the kind of thing I want to see. Creation. God's handiwork. Cities make me feel hemmed in. I like being where there's not so many people."

Hope wondered why he was laying out the apparent differences between himself and Edward. Or were these his perceived differences between her and him? Was he trying to lay his cards on the table? Figure out what the potential for their relationship might be?

Cowell and Len and their violent antics leaped to her mind and she flinched. Would Hope be happy here, in the wilds of the Rocky Mountains? Could she ever feel safe? Did she truly have what it takes to wear the title Frontier Doctor? "I don't miss the city, Lane. Not really. But I might like people just a little more than you do. I know you told me not to think about the what-ifs, but…"

"You still set on leaving?"

"I…I…" Was she? Why was it so hard to say it? *Yes, I'm leaving. I can't make a go of it here. The West is for men or women who can fight and shoot and ride horses.*

Lane moved a little closer. His gaze wandered from her eyes to her lips and back again. "Boy, you confuse me. Make me think about things I didn't think I was ready to think about."

"Like what?"

"Things."

Perhaps she should have been disappointed, but instead, Hope was glad he wasn't speaking his mind. She needed time to ponder *things*, too. He moved closer and she let the kiss happen. His warm, soft lips, his power, his nearness; he overwhelmed her but in the most delicious way. The kiss grew like a wildfire, burning away her wits, her rational thoughts —and then he pulled back, grinning like a man bewildered by a great discovery he didn't know how to rationalize.

Hope sighed and curled up beside him. He put an arm around her and pulled the robe higher. "Warm?"

"Very."

She rested her head on his shoulder and, somewhere in the night, fell asleep. When she woke, the foal had been born. A sorrel colt with a white blaze, he was trying desperately to stand on spindly, shaky legs. After several attempts, he finally made it. Hope looked up at Lane. Smiling from ear to ear, his countenance simply glowed with joy at the scene before them. He looked as if he'd seen the face of God.

In the joy of his simple life, perhaps he had.

———

CHAPTER 7

*C*hristmas Day at the King M ranch was a maelstrom of laughter, music, food, and friendship, and Hope would never forget it. Ranch hands seemed to crawl out of the woodwork. The McIntyre's home was bursting with freshly barbered cowboys in clean clothes, their booming voices bouncing off the polished log walls.

Standing at the head of the long table, Mr. McIntyre blessed the meal with a beautiful prayer, reminding everyone of the special meaning in the day—the Savior's birth. Hope noted how respectfully the men listened, including Lane, and she wondered if he was closer to building a relationship with Jesus than he let on. Mr. McIntyre said *amen* and motioned to the table. No one had to be told twice.

In a matter of minutes, the table, initially set with an abundant supply of food, looked as if a swarm of locusts had passed over it. It had gone far enough, but barely. Hannah and Billy and Little Billy had arrived late, but there was still enough for a full meal. Not much else.

"As long as there's coffee," Billy said, digging into a pumpkin pie, "I'm happy."

One cowboy pulled out his guitar and played Christmas carols as folks finished eating. Those who were done joined him, adding their voices. At home, Hope recalled her father always had a stringed quartet in tuxedoes come and play for the Christmas night party. The music was tasteful and perfectly performed. She preferred, by far, the cowboy's simple but lively presentation of *Jingle Bells* and *God Rest Ye Merry Gentlemen*, with the discordant voices raised in song.

The young guitar player finished with a soft, beautiful rendition of *O Holy Night*, his voice powerful, clear, haunting. His perfectly pitched, crystalline tones stunned the crowd into reverent silence. Then, when the last strum faded, everyone blinked as if they'd been hypnotized and clapped for him with sincere enthusiasm.

"All right, it's time, boys," Lane yelled, stepping up on the hearth, raising himself a few feet over the guests. "Go put on your work duds and meet out at the corral. We're starting off with a bang: bronc ridin'."

Hope had no idea what "bronc ridin'" was, but she grabbed her coat and followed the crowd outside. The ranch hands stampeded toward the bunkhouse, to change she assumed, and Lane and Mr. McIntyre and two other men went into the barn. Naomi tugged her arm and pointed at what looked like newly-constructed, rough-sawn bleachers on the opposite side of the corral.

"Charles had these built for spectators. So, we have a better view of the men breaking their necks."

Hope wasn't really amused and dragged her feet as she walked with Naomi, Hannah, Billy, Ian, and Rebecca toward the seats.

Hannah elbowed her as she shifted Little Billy on her hip. "She was just joking."

"Is it dangerous?"

"Well, yes, but they choose—"

"Excuse me." Hope wouldn't, of course, put a stop to the fun and games, but she changed direction to go find Lane. She headed into the barn and threw herself against the wall with a gasp as a tall, gray mare screamed and reared up.

"Hope, get back," Lane yelled. "What are you doing?" He had a rope around the horse's neck along with a lead rope to the halter. He pulled the horse down, calmed it some, and ran it past her to a chute. He deposited the horse in it, and Mr. McIntyre closed the gate behind the animal. With a quick shake, Lane pulled his rope loose.

Jaw clenched in the first fit of anger Hope had seen him exhibit, he marched toward her, eyes blazing. "There's a reason we built those bleachers over there. For, Pete's sake, what are you doing in the barn?"

Alarmed and embarrassed, Hope tried not to flare up at his anger. He was, after all, somewhat justified. She could have walked right into those flailing hooves. "I'm sorry. I didn't realize and I will be more careful."

Lane dragged a hand over his chin, now sporting a smudge of dirt. "Well, I apologize for getting a little hot with ya. You could've got hurt. If I tell you to go somewhere on this ranch, you go."

"I understand that, but you need to let me help. Lane, I brought my medical bag. What these men are going to do is obviously dangerous. You can't tell me someone won't get hurt today."

"Somebody always gets hurt."

"So…?"

"So…" He pursed his lips and thought about what she was saying. "Yeah, I guess it would be a good idea. All right." He put an arm around her and directed her to the chute. "Go stand on the other side. There's a gate there. Anybody gets hurt, that's where we'll bring 'em through."

She nodded and started off, but then stopped and turned

to him. "Are you participating in this event today or just directing it?"

He slapped his leg with the lariat in his hand. "I'm the first rider."

---

*H*ope's heart was in her stomach as she watched Lane climb aboard the snorting, bucking gray mare that had nearly brained her. All the ranch hands had changed clothes and were either standing at the fence with her, peering into the box containing Lane and the ill-tempered horse, or had taken a seat in the small set of bleachers. Excitement sizzled in the air. Hope clutched her bag and prayed she wouldn't need it, but especially not for Lane.

He wedged his gloved hand tightly into the rigging—the surcingle that circled the horse's girth. He tugged, pulled, tightened it some more and then nodded at Mr. McIntyre with a jerk of his chin. Mr. McIntyre raised his hand, holding a pocket watch. In the other, he held a bell.

Lane's body seemed to vibrate with electricity. He raised one hand in the air, too; the other wedged deeper into the rigging. Hope whispered a prayer as a cowboy snatched a rope and the gate flew open.

Lane and the feisty mare absolutely exploded into the corral. The animal bucked, spun, twisted, side-stepped violently, as if she was furious with Lane for climbing on. Lane stayed on the animal's back almost as if by some miraculous power over the law of gravity. Several times Hope saw daylight between the horse's back and Lane's posterior, but he didn't go anywhere. At one point, the horse bucked so hard and so high, she was nearly vertical, and Hope gasped in terror. Lane was going to die if he didn't get off that animal!

But the cowboys cheered, whistled, clapped, and whooped their support louder and louder the more the seconds wore on.

She wondered how long Lane was expected to stay on when Mr. McIntyre started violently ringing the bell. The crowd roared and cheered its congratulations as Lane released his hand and came flying off the horse. He landed in the snow and dirt first on his feet, but momentum took him to all fours. Quickly, though, he leaped up as another cowboy on horseback swung a rope and brought Lane's mount to a standstill.

The gate opened and the ranch hands congratulated him enthusiastically as he passed through. Grinning like the famed Cheshire Cat, he took the congratulations with good humor but quickly made his way over to Hope. "Now, I'm done."

Hope thought for a moment her knees might buckle. "That was the most terrifying, exciting thing I've ever seen."

She wouldn't have believed it to be possible, but Lane's grin spread. "Yeah, breaks up the boredom of life on a ranch. Keeps us sharp."

She let out a long breath and fell back against the fence. "So very exhilarating. I can tell you, we don't have anything like that in Philadelphia."

"What about you, Johnny Reb?" Lane's gaze had shot past her to Mr. McIntyre strolling by them. "Gonna ride today?"

He drew up, glanced at Hope and shrugged a shoulder. "What for? I've already got my bride."

Hope gasped softly and Lane blushed all the way to the tips of his ears. Laughing with devious delight, Mr. McIntyre resumed walking.

CHAPTER 8

*L*ane rested his gloved hands on the corral rail and let out a breath. It swirled in the dusk's cold air. The quiet of the King M was peaceful, harmonious. Any ranch he'd ever worked, the night of a Christmas rodeo was the quietest of the year. The hands were busy sleeping or nursing injuries. Those who were able nibbled on leftovers.

He grinned at the memories of the day. The laughter. The cheering. A few screams from the ladies. Bawling cattle, neighing horses. Friendship. Community. He was feeling pretty confident he'd made some headway with Hope, convincing her life out here was rough, so were the men, but that didn't mean there was danger around every corner. He'd saved a foal, she had helped, and the boys had been on their best behavior. Surely, he'd proven the worth of the West to her.

He leaned forward and rested his chin on his hands. She'd sure looked as if she was enjoying herself and she'd been grinning ear-to-ear when she rode off with Hannah and Billy. Suppose, though, he did convince her to stay. Might that mean he wanted her to stay…permanently?

He grunted to himself, wishing his ma were here to counsel him. 'Course, he knew what she'd say. *"Pray about it, son. God's got an answer for you—in His time."* He never could understand how his ma had gotten so much from the Lord. She'd heard His voice all the time, it seemed.

He wished she could have met Hope, given Lane her opinion of the good doctor. Sized her up. He would have appreciated her advice.

Troubled by these futile thoughts, he straightened up and rested his hand on the post. It rose up about four inches above the lateral rails and something on this one caught his eyes. A change in color. A little curious, he peered closer. In the fading light, he couldn't be sure, but it looked as if someone had fired a bullet at it. Pulling off a glove and plucking at the splintered wood, he poked and prodded. After a minute, he managed to work free a lead slug.

He bounced it in his hand. Small caliber. .32. Still, shooting a gun off this close to the house and the bunkhouse was pretty stupid. Somebody could have gotten hurt.

He dropped the bullet in his breast pocket beneath his coat and resolved to mention it to the men. Horseplay like that was the kind that got the horse killed...or the man. He couldn't believe someone had been so foolhardy.

---

*H*ope was quite sure she wore a grin all the way back to town that evening. Riding in the back of Hannah's and Billy's wagon, she stared out at the snowy hills framed by the distant mountains, but saw only the day's events. One ridiculously foolish cowboy after another had climbed aboard a bucking horse or an angry bull or grabbed a bull by the horns—quite literally. Some had roped steers in teams or raced their horses around barrels. Anything that could be done on a horse, they did it. As fast as they possibly could.

Hope had treated a few bumps and scrapes, a twisted knee, a broken finger, and a slight concussion. She was amazed the injuries weren't worse or more numerous. Lane had assured her, "These boys know what they're doin'."

The cocky comment made her smile. Men out west seemed to never tire of ways to break up the boredom. Lane had not competed in any other events, and honestly, Hope was glad. He and Mr. McIntyre had managed the events, getting livestock and cowboys into the right places at the right time. And when Lane hadn't been doing that, he'd stood by Hope, either describing the event or assisting with a patient.

All the young men—mostly boys, really—were quite cavalier about their injuries and returned quickly to their competition—

"Do you have plans for tonight, Hope?"

Hannah's question interrupted her musings and she looked at her young aide, twisted on the bench seat, peering back. The suspicion in her raised brow said she wasn't asking merely to be conversational.

"As a matter of fact, no, I do not."

"Oh, you're spending Christmas night—?"

"Alone. You needn't beat around the bush. I told Edward I was sorry, but I felt I'd be getting back too late from the ranch to entertain company. I do feel sorry for him, spending the holiday alone, alone in the office or cooped up in his hotel room. But—"

"You didn't take him to raise." Hannah spun back around in her seat.

Hope had to smile at her euphemism. "No, I did not. He's here uninvited and of his own volition."

A few minutes later, Billy drove the wagon up to the front porch of Hope's little cabin. "Hate to leave you at a cold house, Dr. Clark. I'm sure your fire has gone out. I'd be happy to come inside and build one for you." Billy tugged on the brake and moved to pass the reins off to Hannah.

"Oh, no, don't be silly. I left wood and kindling at the ready. I'll have a fire in a few minutes."

Billy jumped down to assist her from the wagon. "I don't mind, really."

"Nonsense," Hope said, allowing him to lower her to the ground. "You don't need to be putting this wagon and horse up in the dark." And it was getting so quickly. "Get your family home." When he didn't move, she added, "I insist."

Billy scratched his head, mussing his ash blond hair, and frowning. "All right. If you say so." He plucked her carpetbag from the floor of the wagon and escorted her to the door.

W ithout too much delay and just as she had planned, Hope soon had a blazing fire going in her pot-bellied stove. She closed the door and stood up, absorbing the heat while she thought about her life here. For one thing, the idea of moving from Defiance had faded a little today. She'd had such a grand time. The men had been perfect gentlemen. Lane had treated her both like a princess and a doctor, affording her skills great respect.

A shiver shot through, changing the directions of her musings. The little cabin *was* cold. She decided a pot of coffee was more inviting at the moment than a chilled sleeping gown and robe. Changing clothes could wait.

Still holding the box of matches, she strode to the kitchen

counter to light a lantern but froze when she heard a pronounced thud on the front porch. The night she was stabbed rushed back at her with terrifying clarity. The smell of whiskey and Cowell and Len's abhorrent assault reared up as well. She reached out and wrapped her fingers around the lamp. If nothing else, she could certainly use it as a weapon.

Someone knocked on the door. Hope didn't move. Her breathing escalated. Her pulse raced. Surely it was Hannah and Billy. They'd forgotten something.

"Hope, it's me, Edward."

Edward? He sounded strange. Still, Hope relaxed, then irritation set in. She had expressly told him not to come by. Her fear morphing into annoyance, she marched to the door and snatched it open. "Edward, I told you—"

He waved a champagne bottle over his head and clumsily pushed past her into her dim living room. "Say, why's it so dark in here?"

Angry now, Hope shut the door, but only to keep the heat in. She planned on opening it right back up. Edward had been drinking. She'd smelled it as he pushed by; that and the odor of smoke permeated his coat. "Edward, drunk or sober, how dare you presume to come to my home tonight when I told you not to."

He rounded on her, eyes wide and blinking. He stared at her like a confused owl, swaying as he did so. "I presumed because I didn't think you meant it."

"I most certainly did. I'm tired and cold. I've been outdoors all day long treating cowboys at the King M rodeo. I only want to retire. Now, you must leave."

He shook his head and dropped like a rock to her settee. "They told me not to come. Told me not to leave the party."

"They? Party? Where have you been?"

"A group of burly, frontier-types was having a party in the hotel restaurant. They were very generous with their beer.

61

Kegs of it." He waved the bottle. "I brought this for you." He burped. "I apologize for the vintage, but in these—" he burped again—"barbaric conditions, I feel fortunate to have found any champagne at all."

Well, clearly, he had not spent much time in the office. How dare he drink and revel, leaving the town with no doctor.

"What if someone had needed you, Edward? You're quite inebriated." Uncomfortable to be here in the dark with him, Hope lit a lamp and walked it over to the end table beside the couch. "Edward, I'm asking you to leave."

He sighed as if her order took all the wind from his sails. "Fine." He pulled two champagne flutes from his coat. "Have one glass with me and I'll go."

"Where did you get those? Did you take them from the hotel?"

"I did indeed borrow them, but with the very sincere goal of returning them. Share one glass with me and I'll do so straightaway."

"Edward, I—"

"Please?" He waggled the glasses. "Just one and I promise I'll go."

"Very well." She sat down on the settee beside him. A bit swirly, perhaps, he was not sloppily inebriated. He managed with skill to pop the champagne and pour the two flutes. That gave her confidence he would be cooperative and leave after one glass. She should have forced him out without being nice, but just didn't have the strength for the argument.

"What shall we drink to?"

She stared at the glass for a moment and thought about Lane as her breath swirled in the cold room. "To love." She frowned knowing that sounded wrong considering her company, and added, "And friendship."

They sipped and Edward fell back on the furniture, still

in his coat. "So, how was your Christmas out on the range where the deer and the antelope play?" He chuckled at his apparent clever use of the lyrics.

Hope did not lean back. She remained sitting bolt upright and took another sip. "A horse foaled while I was there, and Lane had to help the mare deliver. He was as skilled as any vet. And I found the rodeo quite exciting. No, exhilarating. I loved the way everyone on the ranch came together. There was food and music and then the rodeo. I quite enjoyed myself."

"My, that was a notable Christmas." He sipped the champagne, a discouraged expression on his face, and fell silent. A moment later, "Do you remember the year Princess Helena of Nassau attended your father's party and brought the acting troupe with her?"

"Oh, how could I forget it? They reenacted The Night of Our Savior's Birth. It was beautifully done." At the time, all Hope could think about was how the event would make her father the talk of Philadelphia. Now, she wished she could see the play again to worship Jesus. Oh, how things had changed...

Edward seemed to brighten at her enthusiasm. "She's back in Philadelphia. They're opening St. Bartholomew's Children's Hospital January second."

"Didn't she sell a piece of jewelry to help build it?"

"Donated," he corrected. "Her diamond-encrusted gold brooch paid for over half the building. It was incredibly philanthropic of her. She's a lovely woman. Kind and generous for one so wealthy."

Hope nodded, thinking a children's hospital was a wonderful project. She would donate. It seemed only fitting. After all, she had taken a life—Hope pushed the thought away before it scorched her soul again. She was forgiven and would never, ever repeat the action. Still...it stung.

"You could practice there," Edward said, matter-of-factly.

"What? At St. Bartholomew's?"

"Yes. They need doctors."

"Oh, but I can't go back to Philadelphia as a doctor," she said, drenching her words in sarcasm. "That just wouldn't do."

Edward sighed and took another sip. "You needn't be rude. Yes, I've said you might want to ease patients into accepting you as a doctor. A children's hospital, on the other hand, might not be so picky."

Refusing to have this conversation again, Hope finished off her champagne and set the glass down as hard as she dare without breaking it. "You are ridiculous, Edward. Please finish your drink and go."

He took another sip, but not a large one. "I suppose one could make the argument children wouldn't care if you were a doctor or Merlin the Magician."

"Absolutely. They want only to be made well and to feel safe while they are in the hospital."

"And the parents would most likely agree. You would be a great benefit to them."

He's just giving up the frontal assault. Hannah's words leaped to Hope's mind and she surged to her feet. Was his rude visit here tonight designed to sow more discontent in Hope's heart? Edward didn't know she was contemplating leaving. Was he dangling a children's hospital in front of her like a carrot? Expecting the little ones to tug at her heart-strings. Which they did. It would be a penance of sorts, healing children after taking the life of one—

"You need to leave now, Edward."

Perhaps sensing she was done being polite, he finished his drink, picked up her glass from the table and sighed. "I forgot. I have this for you." He fished in his coat pocket and handed her a small box wrapped in a red ribbon.

"I can't accept—"

"We are old friends, Hope. I hope we will always be so. Please take it."

Eager to get Edward out the door, she opened the box and discovered a silver bracelet with writing on it. In the low light, she couldn't make out the words. "What does it say?"

"But never doubt love." He paused a breath and quoted, "Doubt that the stars are fire, Doubt that the sun doth move his aides, Doubt truth to be a liar…"

"But never doubt love," she finished for him. "Hamlet."

"I mean nothing soulful by it now, of course," he said in a woeful tone, stepping away from her. "Please make sure Mr. Chandler understands that. I have had the bracelet since last winter. I am pleased I was finally able to present it to you."

"It's lovely. Thank you."

Edward ducked his chin, seemed to want to say more, but then excused himself and left. In the quiet room, finally growing warm, Hope realized he'd left the champagne. She laid the bracelet beside it on the table and corked the bottle. It was no use, of course. The drink had lost its effervescence.

CHAPTER 9

For days, the doubts about her pioneering desires —much less skills—wrestled in Hope's mind with her desire to stay in Defiance. She'd had such a joyous day at the McIntyre's ranch. It had planted a seed in Hope's mind that she could learn to ride a horse. It looked so exciting. And terrifying.

Lane's saddle sat in the corner of her living room, mocking her. Was she sturdy enough, brave enough, to handle a horse? He had told her he was looking for just the right animal for lessons. Gentle. Willing.

Idiot proof, in other words. Or, as they say out here, fit for a greenhorn.

Cowell and Len flashed through her mind as she knelt down in front of her stove. *A greenhorn and easy pickings for men intent on violence. What am I doing here?* She pulled her sleeve up high and then tossed another log into the fire. At home in her father's house, servants had done this sort of thing. Even when she'd rented the office space in Denver, the landlord had made sure to build her a fire every morning.

And here she was doing it herself. A simple feat, perhaps,

but she was proud. *I am taking care of myself...*

Her gaze drifted to the saddle. She was afraid of horses. She'd been told they could sense it.

Hope moistened her lips, shook off the concern, and shut the stove door. Rising to her feet, she told herself Lane wouldn't let anything happen to her. He was as comfortable and natural around horses as Hope was around surgical tools. It would be fine.

She prepared breakfast—eggs and bacon—and as she was pulling the items from the stove, Lane knocked on her door. She appreciated that he was punctual.

Wiping her hands on a cloth, she hurried to the door and swung it wide. For an instant, her breath caught. Lane's worn, brown cowboy hat brought out the caramel hints in his blond hair and contrasted invitingly with the brown and green flecks in his eyes—eyes that stared back at her with warmth and affection. She found the sheepskin coat he wore in cold weather so rugged and alluring. He was such a man's man. A cowboy.

A slight smile twitched on his lips as he pulled his hat off. "It's cold out here."

Hope blinked. *What?* "Oh, come in, come in." She stepped aside, her cheeks warming.

He slipped past her, fanning his hat. "You were kinda staring at me like I had two heads."

Hardly. She motioned toward the kitchen table, set with breakfast. "Quite the opposite, actually. May I take your coat?"

Hat and coat set aside, the two settled down for breakfast. Hope felt his stare as she poured his coffee. She had not explained herself and wasn't sure she wanted to.

He tugged the steaming cup a little closer and inclined his head to her. "Something amiss in my appearance? Did I forget to comb my hair?"

Hope laughed softly. "I'm sorry. Sometimes the contrast between you and Edward...catches me off guard."

Lane drummed his fingers on the coffee cup, his brow furrowed. "He and I are about as different as roses and rattlesnakes, I reckon."

Hope couldn't help herself and laughed freely at his way with words. "Remember those stories you told me about your mother?" He nodded. "I could see them. I could see her hunting down the snake that bit your brother. I could see her working your ranch, a baby on her hip. Your words are vivid, Lane. If you weren't a cowboy, I dare say you could be a writer like the Bard."

"I do enjoy Shak—" he bit that off and Hope did not miss the redirection. "Sharing. I enjoy sharing stories about my momma."

"She was quite the pioneer woman," Hope said, her enthusiasm for the day ahead waning.

Lane reached over his plate and patted her hand. "You've got every bit as much grit as she had."

"Oh, I don't know, Lane." She pulled back from the table. "A real pioneer woman wouldn't be afraid to learn to ride a horse."

His head came up. "You shouldn't be afraid. I won't let anything happen to you. Besides, the horse I brought you is the gentlest creature I've ever seen."

"Well, I hope she's also blind in both eyes, deaf in both ears, and crippled in at least two legs."

---

*S*o be it.

Lane finished hobbling Hope's new horse Nancy, buckling the leather strap below the fetlocks, and then stood up. This was an abundance of caution for Hope's sake and he didn't believe the gear would be on the horse for long. "And you're a good gal for puttin' up with this." He patted the buckskin's cheek and then tugged on the saddle again. Everything was to his satisfaction. He unwrapped the reins from around the corral rail and led the horse across the livery's snow-covered round pen to the main gate to wait for Hope.

He'd intended to let her ride Nancy from her home to the pen, but with that comment about the animal being deaf, blind, and crippled, he'd had second thoughts. The last thing he wanted was to scare her off a horse. If she was going to live out here, she needed to know how to ride.

Snow crunched and he looked up. Brow creased with tension, Hope meandered toward him. She had her cashmere coat buttoned up to the very top, her scarf pulled over her nose, and her knit cap pulled down low on her forehead. Even if he couldn't have seen the little v between her eyes, he would have sensed the fear. She grabbed the top rail with fingers swimming in a pair of warm, but thick, wool gloves and exhaled.

"Her name is Nancy," Lane told her. "She's old, wise, and, as you can see, temporarily crippled. You could sleep on her."

Hope cocked her head sideways. "Can she even walk in that thing?"

"That's about all she can do. We won't take it off 'til you say."

Hope squared her shoulders and raised her chin. "All right, then. I'm ready for my first lesson…I suppose."

"There are a lot of things to learn about horses, Hope, like feeding them and caring for them, but I want to get you comfortable with Nancy here, then I'll show you the other things. So, for today, first things first." Lane pulled a pair of small, leather riding gloves from his back pocket. "You have to be able to feel the reins in your hand."

Eyes shining, Hope exchanged gloves and wriggled into them. "These are very nice. Thank you."

Taking her petite, leather-covered hand, he helped her into the saddle and handed her the reins. "Now, a couple of things. First, try to do exactly what I tell you. All right?"

"All right."

"Second, have fun."

She exhaled again. "All right."

He raised a finger. "Sit tight. I'll be right back."

She started to protest as he jogged away, but he had to get something out of his saddlebag hanging on Rusty, his horse. The animal was tied outside the corral. Lane ducked through the rails, fished through the bag, found what he was after and hurried back to Hope. "Take this." He handed her a chipped teacup and saucer.

"What am I supposed to do with these? Make afternoon tea?"

"Hold the saucer in your left hand and the teacup in your right." She dropped the reins and obliged. "No, keep a hold of them."

After an awkward moment finding the right grip, his student sat atop Nancy, the reins and the china in her hands. She shot him a doubtful look.

"I taught my niece to ride this way. Thought it might work for you." He took a step back. "Pretend you've got hot tea in that cup there and you don't want to spill it. Understand?"

"I think so."

The ploy, he'd learned, helped with balance and also kept the student from picking up on too many distractions. "First, we'll just take a few easy turns around the pen. I want you to sit up straight, but don't lean forward."

Lane did not expect to do anything with Hope other than let her stick to the walk. Her balance was pretty loose, and she was afraid to assert herself in the saddle, afraid to believe she could dominate the animal. He suspected she might not do more than walk in the next lesson, as well.

He laid his hand on her lower back, pressed a hand on her thigh, well aware this was not appropriate behavior back East. But they weren't in Philadelphia and she needed to learn this. "Straighten your back, squeeze your legs, don't rely on the stirrups. Lean back a little more. Just a hair." How many times had he told her this?

She sighed in frustration but nodded and gave it a go, once more. Nancy was a trooper, shuffling around the pen, unruffled by the roly-poly human on her back. Hope's balance and movements were coming together with the horse's, but slowly. Lane rubbed his neck, about to call it a day. He didn't want Hope or Nancy to sense his frustration.

"Maybe I should try a trot?"

The request surprised him. "You sure?"

"I'd like to try."

Lane took a deep breath, considering. Nancy had a short, choppy gate, but maybe Hope would get a better feel for the horse's rhythm if it was more pronounced.

Lane fetched a lunge line hanging on the fence, hooked it to the horse's bridle, then squatted down and removed the hobble from Nancy's feet. That done, he winked at Hope and reeled the line out about a dozen feet. "Lean back, to about one o'clock...good...bring your toes up..." Satisfied, he made a *tsk tsk* sound and Nancy responded with a walk. A moment later, Lane repeated it, but faster, and the horse stepped up to a trot. "Lean back, don't come forward," he told Hope. "Don't spill the tea. Keep that cup balanced."

Lane's heart swelled as he watched Hope's fear fade slowly with each trip around the pen. Her tense little pout of concentration changed, softened, melted into a small smile. And then a grin broke free.

As did her concentration. She started sliding to the right. Panic widened her eyes. Lane pulled Nancy to a stop, but not before Hope had tossed the cup and saucer and laid hold of the saddle horn like it was the one thing keeping her from falling off a cliff.

"Oh, I'm sorry," she fussed, righting herself in the saddle. "I don't know what happened—"

"Don't worry about it," Lane said soothingly. "You were doing well. You'll be riding like a cowboy in no time."

"I don't know what happened, but I nearly fell off."

"Just lost your balance, is all. Nothing a little more practice won't fix."

She shifted again, lifting her bum from the saddle. "I should think I could do better."

She sounded disgusted. Lane unhooked the lunge line from Nancy and grinned up at Hope, trying to encourage her and not have this end on a sour note. "You're nervous. That's all. When you get more used to her, it'll all settle. You'll find your seat—"

Without any warning, Nancy bucked and screamed. Hope went flying and Lane's heart shot to his mouth. She cartwheeled backward to the ground, planting her face in the snow and the dirt with an audible thud. Nancy was high-stepping toward the corral gate like a wolf was nipping at her heels.

Lane dropped to his knees beside Hope, his throat knotting up with fear. "Hope, Hope, are you all right?" He knew better than to touch her just yet.

She mumbled something, raised her head, and spit out a mouthful of dirt and snow. He gently drifted his hands down her back. "Anything hurt?" He touched the lower part of her spine, her hips. "Anything broke?" His heart was hammering in his chest. *Dear God, please don't let her be hurt.* "I don't know what could have made her spook like that."

Hope pushed to all fours and looked at her imprint in the snow. "What happened?" She flinched and touched her forehead. "Oh, my head..." She paled in color and Lane knew a headache was blooming in her skull. Severe enough, it might even make her vomit.

Somewhere off to his right, outside the corral, the ring of mean-spirited laughter touched his ears. Fury arced in him and Lane half-rose but didn't leave her. A group of ill-mannered young boys was scattering into the trees on the edge of the corral. "Hey, you kids, I catch you you're gonna think the end of the world has come!" He sounded livid but softened his tone when speaking to her. "Kids and snowballs. I catch 'em, I'll string 'em up from a lamp post...You sure you're okay?"

"Yes, I just need a moment." She groaned and then nodded. "I think it's fading." She breathed slowly, purposefully. Finally, she could stand and Lane helped her to her feet. Clutching his hand, she nodded. "The nausea and the light-headedness is passing."

Lane was incensed at the little hoodlums, but concerned for Hope at the same time. Not just for her physical condition, but for her state of mind after this. "I'm sorry, Hope. You can't imagine how terrible I feel. This should have never happened. I see those kids again..."

"It's certainly not your fault," she said, rotating her head around and rubbing the base of her neck.

"Goes to show, you should always be on your guard. I'm sorry I didn't see those little devils. And they'd better hope they never see me again."

"I'm quite sure hiding was their intent."

"I'll see 'em again. Kids like that don't stay outta trouble long."

Hope slid her gaze over to Nancy. The horse watched them with boredom, ears flicking around, the reins dangling to the ground. Hope's face tensed, her eyes widened. "I could have broken my neck."

Lane's heart sank. The worst thing possible had happened —an accident on her first lesson. That would be tough to overcome.

"I think I'm done for the day," she said distantly.

"For the day," he agreed. He didn't tell her she'd need to try again. If she didn't, she might never ride.

"Oh, it was…" Hope shook her head as she helped Hannah make up a bed. "I can't describe it. I was riding a horse. A huge, powerful animal and I steered him… and…we trotted…"

"But?"

"I can understand the exhilaration of it. It is quite freeing. But it was also—I was so nervous the whole time. And then those vile boys had to show up."

"That was unfortunate, but at least you didn't get hurt."

"Yes. At least." And she could have. So easily. The thought made her stomach flutter.

"Naomi wasn't very good when she first started riding. Now she loves it. In fact, she's quite skilled at it."

Another concern crossed Hope's mind. "Surely, she's not riding anymore. Not until the baby comes?"

"I've told her. You've told her. Charles has told her." Hannah fluffed the pillow and centered it at the head of the narrow bed.

"And we're all assuming she's listening?"

"Yes."

"And Naomi is good about this sort of thing?"

Hannah opened her mouth, closed it, shook her head. "I

suspect she was riding some before Christmas, but I don't think she is now."

"Let's hope she's sticking to the wagon. But I can certainly see how quick and agile a person could be responding to emergencies on horseback, especially in difficult locations or far out from town. A single horse is faster than a wagon. But it terrifies me, the thought of riding out alone."

"Well, don't worry too much about it. The more you're around horses, the less they'll scare you."

"So, you went through with it?" Edward's highly disapproving tone brought them both up short. But Hope would not allow herself to be bullied by this interloper. She turned to find him standing in the room's doorway. He immediately started unbuttoning his coat with short, angry motions.

"Yes, I am taking riding lessons. Lane is teaching me. And I'm keeping my horse down at the livery."

"Good Lord, Hope, have you no idea how dangerous this is? You could be thrown and seriously injured. Killed even."

She and Hannah exchanged quick, guilty glances, but Hope rushed past it. "I could slip in the snow and break my neck. Life is a gamble, Edward." Whether she ever sat in the saddle again was irrelevant. She wouldn't be talked to like a child.

A sigh escaped him that was more like a growl and he dragged a hand over his mouth. "If you won't think of yourself, think about the town. If you get hurt, we're down a doctor. I can ride. I can take calls that might require one to saddle up, as they say."

Hope wanted to tell him she hoped he wouldn't be around much longer to respond to such calls, but bit her tongue. Especially since she might not, either. The riding lesson had choked her with fear. It was a wonder she was able to keep the tremor from her voice when she'd been talking to Lane.

"I find it highly irresponsible of Mr. Chandler to teach you. Doesn't he care if you get hurt?"

"That's why he's teaching me, Edward. He's teaching me to ride safely and wisely. Skillfully." Short of the children with slingshots, the lesson would have been perfectly mundane. Most likely her last as well, but she wouldn't admit it aloud.

The young doctor's pale cheeks flamed red and his mouth tightened into a grimace. "I say again, I think this is foolish." With that, he spun and marched across the office. The girls jumped at the door to the other examination room slamming shut.

"I suppose he does have your best interests at heart," Hannah offered gently.

"So does Lane. He wants me to be able to see a patient anytime, anywhere." The difference in the two men's attitudes was striking.

Hannah strolled to the end of the bed and picked up the dirty sheets. "Hope, are you prepared to get back in the saddle?"

"You say it as if it's inevitable."

"They say, when you get thrown, you have to get right back on the horse."

Hope didn't want to hear this. She wanted to imagine Lane teaching her to ride well and nothing like this would ever happen again. She wouldn't ride insanely fast or in places where only experienced riders should go. Her riding forays would be calm, predictable, sensible.

Or maybe she'd just take the train back to Philadelphia and ride in carriages for the rest of her life.

CHAPTER 10

"I'm sorry, she's not here, Lane." Hannah shrugged with the apology.

Somehow, he knew it when he stepped into the office. "She be back any time soon?"

"I don't think so. She went over to Mrs. Raye's to deliver her baby. She could be quite a while. Edward is at the mine tending to an injured man."

"Yeah, I hate I missed him."

Hannah chuckled at the jab.

"I just wanted to say hi before I rode over to Ruby City." He twirled his hat in his hands, truly sorry to have missed Hope. "Long, cold ride. I was gonna ask her if she might feed me supper on my way back through this evening."

"You're more than welcome to join Billy and me and warm up. Spend the night if you want."

Lane considered it. "I'll take you up on the offer of food. Then I'll see if I warm up, and just how lumpy your settee is."

Hannah snorted. "If you're half-frozen when you come back, I'll make you eat those words."

Lane dropped his hat in place. "You just might." He

winked cheerfully. "I'll see you this evening. Thank you for the offer."

"And I'll be sure to invite Hope."

Lane reached for the door, but instead of turning the knob, rested his hand on it. He hadn't ever been good at this sort of thing—reading a woman. Especially the top-shelf ones.

"Yes?" Hannah coaxed.

Slowly, Lane turned to face her. "I'm stumped, Hannah. I don't know how to tell the difference between love and a passing flirtation." Hannah's eyes bugged and Lane felt like a fool. But if the accident with the horse had pushed Hope away, Lane wanted to know how to handle things. Namely, whatever he was feeling for the woman.

"You think you might be in love with Hope?"

Again, a yea or a nay didn't feel right. He just didn't know his own mind and found that pretty dang frustrating. He didn't really want to discuss it with Hannah, either, her being so young and all. Why had he even brought this up? But she worked so closely with Hope every day.

"I know this," she said, surprising him with confidence in her voice as she rose from her desk. "She's over the moon for you but worries you might be dallying with her. On top of that, she's trying to figure out if she really belongs here."

"Of course she does."

"I agree. She's as much of a pioneer woman as my sisters and I were when we first came to Defiance. We had a lot of learning to do, too. Including better horseback riding skills. Most importantly, though, we had to be willing to put down roots."

"Roots?"

"I think you can help Hope with that part, but don't do it if you don't mean it. In my opinion, you're either dallying or...running scared."

The pointed remark stung, and Lane's spirit bucked up. "Thank you for your insight." He wanted to argue he wasn't scared of anything but a stampede of Texas Long Horns, but instead slipped outside and shut the door firmly behind him.

"Running scared," he scoffed as he stepped into the saddle and turned Rusty away from the Doc's office.

A keen, bright sun lit the road out of Defiance, the glare off the knee-deep snow nearly blinding. Lane and Rusty traveled at a steady pace, but the horse couldn't make the time he had hoped, the icy ruts making the journey grueling. When they came to the short cut, he turned the horse off the wagon road and headed up the trail. Steeper than the main thoroughfare and it required one stream crossing, but he figured it could save him two hours. Several folks had been through already and busted a path.

Rusty upped his pace and it wasn't much past noon when they reached the Spanish Fork, a lazy tributary to the Animas, about thirty feet from bank to bank. It was also frozen solid. "Dang," Lane whispered, instantly dismounting. "Is what it is. Come on, boy."

A snow-covered sheet of ice, it looked as though several horses had been across it today, though in widely varying paths. *Avoiding thin ice?* He wondered.

He sucked on his teeth, surveying the stream. Most of the tracks veered up to the right, making an arc to the other side. Only a few tracks went straight across.

"Somebody must suspect the ice has gotten thin in the middle, pard." Rusty grumbled as if answering. "Well, we ain't turning back." He stared hard at the stream. It made sense to cross where others had made it. "We'll do this slow and easy."

Lane led Rusty behind him and stepped out on the ice.

Nothing creaked. He listened intently to the frozen sheet beneath his feet as he and Rusty carefully made their way across. When they neared the center of the stream, the ice began to moan and crackle. Lane wasn't necessarily alarmed. Ice was always thinner in the middle, but he tugged Rusty onward, moving a touch faster.

Only a dozen or so feet from the shore, all hell broke loose. There had been a sound, but before he could focus on it, the world was snatched out from under his feet. The ice cracked, then shattered in an explosion of what sounded like a chandelier crashing to the ground.

Rusty let loose with a shrill, piercing scream, pawing madly at anything solid, but the ice was moving, buckling beneath them. Viciously frigid water surged over Lane, so cold it stole his breath, and blackness wrapped around him like the icy grip of death.

Hope had never experienced such bone slicing fear. Corky and Dub burst into her office, carrying an unconscious Lane between them wrapped in a blanket. "Oh, dear Lord, what's happened?" She rushed to them, her heart in her throat. Lane was pale blue, his lips bluer still, and his skin was like ice. "Quickly, bring him in here." She surged ahead of them, yelling, "Hannah, heat some bricks." Where was the girl?

Hannah burst from the other room and gasped at the sight of Lane's condition. "On it."

Hope jerked the quilt out of the way and assisted as the men laid Lane on the bed. His clothes were frozen, his hair was a mass of icicles. She didn't bother to check his pulse. He was alive and had to get warm as fast as possible. "Thank you, gentlemen. I'll take it from here. Please help Hannah heat some bricks."

Wide-eyed with concern, the men nodded and shuffled out. Moving as if her own life was at stake, Hope jerked Lane's boots off, then started unbuttoning his shirt, practically tearing through the buttons. She sat him up and grunted with the effort of trying to control his limp body, working up a sweat. She moved him from side to side, clinging to his leaden body as she worked his arms free of the flannel. *Dear Lord, give me the strength to do this. I had no idea he'd be so heavy...*

She let him fall back as she worked on his breeches. Lane's pants came off easier, but the damp long johns beneath were thinner, clinging stubbornly to his body. She attempted to sit him up again, hoping to make the process easier, but he was like moving a water-logged bag of flour. She grunted and tugged, desperately trying to hold him up and get the clothes off at the same time.

Edward came in, assessed the scene and jumped in to assist. "Why didn't you call for help, Hope?" His tone was accusatory. "This would have gone much faster with the two of us."

She wiped sweat from her brow and immediately regretted the action, which arguably proved his point. Edward glared at her as he tugged one of Lane's arms free. "He has a good seventy-five pounds on you and he's dead weight."

"Don't say that," she said, finally working the undergarment free from Lane's upper torso. Tugging on it as Edward lifted Lane, she worked it free, tossing it aside, and then pulled the quilt back over their patient. Hannah appeared with a brick wrapped in a towel. Hope waved her in. "We need to get his torso warm first." She took the brick and shoved it under the covers. "Keep them coming."

Edward was already checking Lane's pulse at his wrist and had his stethoscope pressed to the patient's heart. "Hmm. Weak, but alive. We need to get him warm. Time is of the essence."

The three of them worked quickly to raise Lane's body temperature; Hope all the while on the verge of tears. She waged a valiant struggle to keep her emotions hidden, especially from Edward, but fear and guilt assailed her. Yes, she should have called for Edward immediately. Hope knew Lane would be heavy, but she'd been convinced she could maneuver him. A woman doctor alone in the frontier would most likely be forced to manhandle patients much heavier than herself.

But today she wasn't alone. And she should have asked for help. The difference in Lane living or dying quite literally could rely on mere seconds. She shoved another warm brick down at his feet and finally had the control to ask Hannah, "What happened? Do we know?"

"Corky and Dub saw Rusty wandering down the road without Lane, so they took off toward Ruby City. Found him lying on the side of the creek, half of him still in the water."

"Dear God," Hope croaked. "He could have died. Hypothermia is deadly."

Hannah squeezed her shoulder. "Yeah, but he's a Texan."

The joke, intended to ease the tension, almost made Hope sob. Biting her bottom lip, she nodded, but couldn't respond. Texan or not, he wasn't immortal.

They stuffed more bricks around him, rotated the cool ones out, covered him in multiple quilts, laid warm towels on his head, and prayed. So afraid for Lane, Hope nearly climbed in the bed with him. If Edward hadn't been here, she thought she might have done just that.

After a while, Edward once again checked Lane's pulse, then reached under the warm towel on his head and touched his scalp. "Heartbeat's a little stronger and his body temperature is rising. We need to keep rotating in warm bricks, Hannah, and let's try to rouse him. Maybe get some broth in him."

"Certainly." Hannah scurried from the room.

"His hair is still damp, Hope. Why don't you dry it and I'll get another warm towel?"

Hope moved instantly and began gently rubbing Lane's scalp and scrunching his hair in the towel. "Please wake up," she whispered, close to his face. "Wake up." *Oh, God, let him wake up.* "You're a Texan, remember."

---

CHAPTER 11

*A*woman in a black gown stood still as death in the dusty street, her face hidden behind a lace mantilla. Wind swirled in the ruffles at her skirt, fluttered in the black veil. The traditional peineta pinned in her hair gave her head the unmistakable shape of a Spanish noblewoman. As a tumbleweed rolled in front of her, she clutched the veil with a bony hand, preparing to raise it, reveal her identity.

Icy fingers of dread slithered up Lane's backbone. He did not want to see the face. This woman was evil. She carried the stench of death on her; it surrounded her in the wind.

Suddenly, gunfire erupted around him. Texas Rangers on fire-breathing steeds thundered down the street, shooting into windows, down alleys, behind hay bales. Glass shattered and caballeros tumbled from the second stories of buildings. Some staggered from the shadows into the street, collapsing in pools of blood at the woman's feet.

She, however, remained perfectly still, fiercely immovable, except for the hand lifting the veil. It revealed deep-set, dark eyes, almost black with rage. They glared at Lane from an ancient, wrinkled face sagging with bitterness.

Swansboro all over again. The thought knifed through him.

A young boy, a teenager, appeared over the old woman's shoulder. Lane could see the family resemblance, especially in the way he, too, glared with murderous intent.

"He will kill you," the old woman said, her voice an evil hiss. "He will avenge my son."

Before Lane could respond, a wall of water exploded from behind the pair, slamming into him. An unimaginable, breath-stealing cold swallowed the world, swirled around him, crushed his lungs as if he were in the mouth of a bear. Desperation and panic stole his reason. Air. He needed air. He clawed and flailed madly at the ice filling his lungs—

"Lane, Lane. It's all right."

Hope?

A hand pressed down gently on his chest forcing him back. "You're here in the office. You're safe now."

He took a long, glorious breath and calmed his fears, drifting away from the icy water to a fog of warm exhaustion. Still, her voice compelled him to open his eyes. The effort it took stunned him. Finally, he focused on her beautiful, angelic face hovering over him. And he knew he was all right.

"Lane." She touched his cheek and smiled. "Everything's fine." She turned and called over her shoulder. "Hannah, don't let Mr. McIntyre leave. Lane's awake."

"Barely," Lane said, but he croaked the words in a dusty whisper.

Hope brought a cup of warm broth to his lips. "Here, you need this." She helped him take a sip and when he leaned back, Charles was standing at the end of his bed, hands tucked in his pockets, a mischievous grin on his face.

"You want some time off to be around the lady doctor, you could just ask."

"Very funny, Johnny Reb." He flinched at his dry throat

and Hope helped him with another sip. He lay back, over-whelmed by the fatigue. He'd never been this tired in his life. Not even after a cattle drive. "What the heck happened?"

"You don't remember?" Hope leaned in a little closer, that pinch in her brow showing.

He closed his eyes and thought for a minute. Leading Rusty across the stream. Cracking sounds. Biting, vicious ice water surrounding him. He looked up at her. "My horse?"

"He's fine," Charles answered for her. "Corky and Dub saw him on the road without you and knew something had gone wrong. So, once more, do you remember what happened?"

"Yeah, we were on the way to Ruby City, crossing the stream—" A cracking sound. Different from the sound of the ice, but at almost the same time. Which sound had come first? Was he even remembering right? Or had he imagined it?

"What?" Charles asked.

Should he even voice it? Maybe it was a far-fetched idea. Sleep pulled at him, but he forced his eyes a little wider. "Hope, you mind letting me and Charles talk?"

"Of course not." The pinch in her brow was still there as she rose and left the room.

Charles glanced over his shoulder, as if to make sure the door was shut, then came back to Lane. "What is it?"

"Probably nothing, but I don't reckon I'm one to imagine the sound of a rifle, either."

"A rifle?"

Talking was becoming unimaginably difficult, but he had to get this out. "The bullet...the bullet I found in the corral fence post..." he closed his eyes and faded off.

Charles touched his shoulder. "Try to tell me, Lane."

He blinked, struggling to reject the siren song of sleep.

"None of the boys 'fessed up… and I think somebody took a shot at me … on the trail…"

Too much. He had to sleep.

---

*H*ope watched over Lane like a mother hen. He slept peacefully, barely moving, for a solid day. Biting her bottom lip, she reached over and tucked the quilts a little tighter around him and then sat down again.

Why didn't you call for help, Hope?

She flinched at the scolding. Edward was so right. What had she been thinking? She blinked back tears, sick over her ridiculous ideas. A city girl, trying to make her way in the Wild West. This was no place for her.

She could have killed Lane simply by the delayed response. Such foolishness. Trying to prove herself.

She squeezed her eyes shut and fought back the tears, the guilt, the hissing voice of failure. Once more she'd made a decision that had not been in the best interest of a patient. Just like Mary Ann and a surgery that had killed her. *Oh, Lord, when will I ever learn?*

"Hey," Lane whispered softly as he lay his hand upon hers. "Those tears for me?"

She wrangled back a sob, but barely. Her chin quivered and a trickle ran free from her eyes. Hope wiped at them angrily and shook her head. "I can't do this, Lane. I don't know what I was thinking. I don't belong here."

"Oh. That. 'Cause of the horse?"

"They brought you in here nearly frozen to death and I couldn't even lift you once they left you in the bed. It was all I could do to get you out of your wet clothes. If Edward hadn't helped—"

"I reckon you might coulda got me undressed eventually." He wiggled his eyebrows, trying to make a joke.

"You don't understand. Time was of the essence. I wasted precious minutes trying to handle the situation myself and you could have died."

"Ah, a little cold water wasn't gonna hurt me. Us Texans—"

"Oh, stop it with the tall tales. Lane, your pulse was barely there. Your respiration was fading. You could have died in my arms...while I was trying to prove a woman can be a doctor alone on the frontier. I should have called for Edward immediately."

Lane waited a moment, then let out what sounded to her like a resigned sigh. "I don't know what to say." He shook his head. "I know the most important thing in the world to you is helping folks. And you're a good doctor. I know how frustrating it is to want to do a job and something keeps getting in the way."

"If I'd only been the son my father wanted."

"That's hogwash. Pardon me for sayin' so. A man has limitations, too, Hope. Eventually, we all need to ask for help."

She supposed he was right, but at the moment she simply felt so defeated and so...incapable.

Lane stared somberly at his hands and spoke in a calm, gentle, but sad voice. "If you want to leave, if that will make it better, easier for you to practice medicine, if that's what you want, then that's what you should do."

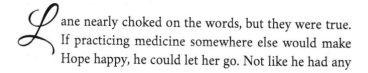

ane nearly choked on the words, but they were true. If practicing medicine somewhere else would make Hope happy, he could let her go. Not like he had any choice.

"What about you, Lane? What do you want?"

Hope stared at him with eyes so intense and blue a September sky paled in comparison. She seemed to be asking more than the question on the surface and he didn't know what to say aloud. She confused him. He'd rather cut off his right arm than see her leave…but he'd do the same thing if it would bring her some happiness.

"I want you to be happy." He thought about the observation that had sort of slipped out on its own. It felt right. "That much, at least, I know."

"So, you'd be," she swallowed, "all right if I left?" She spoke haltingly, as if she couldn't find the right words. "I mean, you wouldn't miss me?"

He took her hand. "Your future is settled, Hope. You're a doctor. You can help people. Save lives." He shrugged a shoulder. "I run cattle. And I like what I do. I would miss you more than I could ever say—" He paused, wondering why that was so. Why couldn't he just stumble through explaining his tangled emotions and see what she did? In the end, however, he didn't. "You have to do what you have to do."

A sad little smile tweaked her lips, and she jerked her chin in a curt nod. "I have to check on another patient. I'll be back."

For a long while after she left, Lane wondered about his heart. A word kept bubbling up in his mind when he was around Hope, but he wouldn't let it break the surface. That one little word got a lot of men in trouble. Broke a lot of hearts. It was not a thing to be dallied with. Besides, he didn't think it was enough to keep Hope here.

On the unlikely chance he wanted her to stay for serious reasons and she returned these serious reasons—what would things look like between them five, ten years down the road? Would she wind up regretting her choice to practice medicine in a hardscrabble mining town or the lonely, windswept hills of Texas? Would she resent Lane for holding her back?

No, love was just too terrifying to bring into this story. Hope had to be free to make her choices for her reasons.

He scrubbed his face and huffed an angst-laden sigh. He had to get out of here, get a good, strong horse beneath him, and ride hell-bent for leather across a snowy pasture. Then all would be right in his world. He tossed the quilts off him and rose to his feet.

*L*ane was prepared to rent a pretty sorry nag from the livery, when Bob the owner came out of the barn, trailing Rusty behind him. Lane felt the grin explode on his face. "Why ain't he back at the ranch?"

Bob chuckled. "Corky dropped him off. Said you'd be wanting him in a day or two. If anything changed, he'd let me know."

Lane certainly had never wanted to kiss a man, but if Corky had been standing nearby at that moment, he might would have got a surprise peck on the forehead. "God love that little fella."

"Yeah, he said he thought this would make your day. Want me to saddle him for ya?"

"Nah. I'm good. Just got a little cold was all."

Bob pushed his thinning, wispy hair back over his head and squinted at Lane. "He was concerned. Said you were a snowflake shy of being a permanent icicle."

"Eh," Lane waved away the suggestion and took the lead rope from Bob. "Corky exaggerates. It's his gift. I'll saddle my own horse."

*L*ane was about half mile out of town and about to kick Rusty up from the trot to a canter, when he tugged on the reins and brought the horse to a stop. An idea nagged at him. He glanced up at the sun, hanging high in the sky. He had time. And he needed to know for sure. He spun Rusty and headed back in the direction from whence they'd come.

The weather was warmer today, and the sun was melting the snow off the trees. Wet clumps of white were falling off the pines in great, crashing cascades. Eventually, they came to the fork and he directed Rusty up the Ruby City short cut. Within minutes they were staring at the stream, still frozen, but there was ragged, choppy evidence of the break the day before yesterday.

Lane dismounted and led Rusty over to a tree. He wrapped the reins around a branch and patted his horse on the nose. "You stay here—and I'm puttin' you on a diet when we get back."

For a few minutes, Lane stood on the edge of the water and studied the banks. The other side was steeper, higher, afforded a better view of the crossing. "And that's where I'd be if I wanted to shoot somebody."

With great care, Lane crossed the ice, but his weight didn't even make the ice creak. He gazed up the hill, into the thin woods, appraising the topography with the mind of a sniper. A boulder, about a hundred yards up caught his eye. High ground. Good camouflage. Safe.

He started up toward it, the snow, knee-high, wet and heavy, soaking his pants, chilling his toes. Just as he suspected, the view of the crossing from the boulder was more than adequate for a good shot. He leaned on it and sighted an imaginary rifle.

Bullet would have gone into the water. Whoever it was, he was a mighty poor shot. He shouldn't have missed—

The ice.

Had the ice broken right at the moment—

That was crazy.

Maybe I'm imagining all this. He looked up at the sky, kinda, sorta talking to God. *Am I?*

Only silence filled the blue expanse.

Drumming his fingers restlessly on his thigh, he tried to recall the incident in the stream. It seemed maybe Rusty's step had stuttered, the horse had hesitated. Maybe he'd heard a sound, a rifle cocking? Or had he sensed the ice about to break? Aggravated, Lane pinched the bridge of his noise. Was he even remembering right?

He just didn't know.

He bent down and brushed the snow back where he would have stood had he been on a hunt but found nothing. He spent another half hour kicking and digging snow out of the way. No shell casing, no footprints, nothing. The snow was deep, and the ground was frozen. It would be easy to miss something.

But, no, he finally came to believe he'd imagined the sound of a rifle firing. Maybe the cracking ice had just triggered something in his brain, brought to life a memory from his own sniper days. Heck, he still had occasional nightmares. He wasn't over the War Between the States by a long shot.

He *tsked* thoughtfully, then nodded. Yeah, just his mind playing games with him. He brushed some snow off his gloves and headed back toward Rusty.

CHAPTER 12

*L*ane picked up the ledger from his small, cramped desk in his room in the bunkhouse and wandered out to the main room. All the men were out, ignoring the snow and the cold and doing their jobs. Glad for the quiet, he pulled a chair closer to the big buck stove that heated the place and tried again to make sense of the numbers so he could talk intelligently about them.

But his attention span was about that of a baby duck. No. Right now, a baby duck was probably capable of more focus than he was. Lane couldn't keep his mind from wandering back to Hope. Funny, without any effort at all, his thoughts drifted to her. He'd be imagining sharing a thought or idea with her before he realized it. Or be revisiting their last conversation. She was thinking about leaving. He had the sense he should have made a bolder declaration about her staying. Telling her she had to do what she had to do hadn't been exactly the right thing to say. But what else could he say? She had to make her own choices.

And he'd gone and done it again. Thinking about her—

"A man with such a pensive dip in his brow..." Charles'

soft Southern tones brought Lane's head back to the moment. "Can only be thinking of a woman." Charles spun a chair away from the wall and straddled it.

Lane didn't even feel like trying to deny the accusation. He sighed and rested his hand on the page. "She does seem to be interfering some in my work here."

A devilish glint in his dark eyes, Charles folded his arms on the top of the chair and rested his chin on them. "Don't let her go if she matters to you. Lay your cards on the table."

Problem was, Lane didn't exactly know what kind of hand he was holding. He didn't respond aloud and after a moment, Charles changed the subject. "On that other matter, have you determined whether you heard a shot or not, when you were on your way to Ruby City?"

"About that…" Lane mentally retraced his investigation. "Nothin'. I'm inclined to think maybe I'm not the scout I used to be."

Charles chewed on his bottom lip for a moment, considering. "If you're satisfied, I will be as well."

Satisfied? Lane wasn't sure he'd go that far—

"Señor Charles! Señor Charles!" Maria's panicked, screeching cries brought both men to their feet. The woman burst into the room, a bloody towel in her hand. "Señora Naomi, it is her time. She say get the doctor. Pronto!"

Before Charles could turn to him, Lane was moving. "I'll fetch her."

---

*H*ope flipped through the medical textbook listlessly. Some of the miners were presenting with unusual respiratory symptoms and she suspected a gas leak in the Sunnyside Mine might be the problem, but it was only a theory. A theory that couldn't hold her attention.

For two days she'd been preoccupied—embarrassingly so —with Lane's willingness to let her leave Defiance. And then he had just up and slipped out without so much as a by-your-leave. What was going on in the man's head? Was he glad she wanted to leave Defiance? Was he glad to be freed from the encumbrance their relationship seemed to be building? In reality, perhaps he truly did not want any long-lasting romantic entanglement. He had been dallying, after all.

She sighed and Hannah heard the sound as she closed a door behind her. "Want to talk about it," she asked, hugging a tray to her chest.

"Not really."

This time, Hannah sighed and walked over to the chair in front of Hope's desk. "I have a theory." She sat down and Hope looked up, waiting, without any enthusiasm.

"I think Lane is in love for the first time in his life and I think it scares him. I also think he's afraid of you choosing to stay when you feel you should go."

"So, you agree. I should leave Defiance?"

"Absolutely not. We need you here, Hope. Edward isn't going to stay. He hates it here. He's miserable. Between the two of you, you are the one with the grit to make it work. But you have to believe in yourself."

"I've made so many mistakes."

"I could write a book on all the mistakes Naomi, Rebecca, and I made when we first came here. You live. You learn. If you would stop looking at your failures and focus on your successes, I think you'd really come to understand the way the challenges have brought out the best in you."

Hope tapped her pencil on the patient's file in front of her, unconvinced. Her successes felt so few and far between. "I also have a theory. I think he would prefer to remain a free-roaming cowboy with the ability to come and go as he pleases. He talks often of Texas. He misses it and is looking forward to his trip there in the spring. When he meets the right woman, Hannah, I'm convinced she'll be the pioneer stock you think you see in me."

"So, does that mean you've made up your mind?"

Had she? Why did her heart cry out to talk this over with Lane? He'd made things pretty easy for her, in reality. "Not a hundred percent, no, but I am leaning toward it."

Hannah's lips moved like she wanted to say more, but she finished with, "Well, I'm done for the day. I'll see you in the morning."

A headache pulsing behind her eyes, Hope wished her a good evening and then buried her head in her hands. She could go home, too, but wasn't in the mood to face a cold, empty cabin yet. There was paperwork to do. A squeak in the chair brought her head up and she found herself staring into Edward's gleaming amber eyes. His countenance seemed alight with victory as he pushed a stray curl off his forehead.

"What, Edward?" Hope asked, assuming he'd heard the whole conversation with Hannah.

"I couldn't help but overhear. I must say, you give me grounds to hope." He chuckled. The pun always made him laugh, even as it annoyed her.

"Hope for us?"

"No, of course not. I was thinking of St. Bartholomew's and all the children who could benefit from your loving, skilled, compassionate care." Hope raised a hand to stop him, but he rushed on. "Think of it, Hope. Patients the perfect size for a woman of your genteel stature."

Her mouth fell open. She couldn't actually decide what offended her more—Edward's blatant demeaning point, or the pure, accurate logic of it. Children. Yes, in most cases, certainly easier for a woman to handle than an unconscious, one-hundred-and seventy-five-pound man.

And she loved children. Hope deflated, too weary of this

argument to carry it forth. Edward shifted in the chair, leaning back and crossing his legs. "You'd certainly be a blessing to the little ones. Oh, how they'd adore you. No one can resist you. Look how your patients here love you."

"Edward, I'm tired. I'll be turning in —"

"I'm sure you'll miss your handsome, exciting cowboy, but, well…"

"What?"

"In the end, you're not suited to this life. You're certainly not suited to the life of a cowboy's wife. Besides—well, I overstep. My apologies."

"Oh, don't stop now, Edward. I need the benefit of your wisdom. Hannah has shared her perspective on my love life. Why not you?"

He paused, then shifted again, finally uncrossed his legs and leaned toward her. "Hope, when a man is in love, really in love, he doesn't run from it."

"I suppose I would be inclined to agree."

<hr />

*L*ane dropped Rusty at the livery and asked Bob to hook up a rig for the doctor. Then he hot-footed it over to Hope's. They were going to have to get a move on. The snow was coming down hard and cutting visibility. They for sure needed to be at the ranch before dark.

His hand on the doorknob, he paused when he heard Edward and Hope talking. He didn't mean intentionally to eavesdrop, at first. But the conversation brought him to a standstill.

"In the end, you're not suited to this life. You're certainly not suited to the life of a cowboy's wife. Besides—oh, I overstep. My apologies."

"Oh, don't stop now, Edward. I need the benefit of your

wisdom. Hannah has shared her perspective on my love life. Why not you?"

"Hope, when a man is in love, really in love, he doesn't run from it."

The pause waiting for Hope's response nearly brought an impatient growl from Lane.

"I suppose I would be inclined to agree."

The whole conversation had hit him like a freight wagon, but that last—his gut ached from the physical kick of it. Something in his soul roared in anger, and he wanted to punch Edward so hard the man would wake up in the next century.

I am not afraid of love. I am not...I'm...

Supposed to fetch the doctor, a distracting voice bellowed in his head.

Lane sucked it up and burst into the office. "Naomi's in labor and she's asking for you, Hope."

She launched to her feet. "I'll get my bag."

As Hope dashed about grabbing her things, Lane and Edward locked challenging gazes. Edward knew Lane had heard at least the last part. Lane was sure of it.

---

CHAPTER 13

*H*ope was disturbed by Edward's fiery darts that pierced her soul. She was distracted by them and found the buggy ride out to the King M with Lane….awkward. Tense. Neither of them spoke of anything but Naomi and the impending birth. She wanted desperately to ask him why he had slipped out of the office without a good-bye, but Edward's stinging comments forced her to veer away from the subject.

Lane, himself, offered very little conversation as well. The distance between them seemed as wide as a continent and Hope felt as if it was forcing her away, as well.

Night had fallen by the time they reached the ranch and she and Lane both were nearly frozen. Regardless, Hope left her coat at the front door and raced to Naomi's bedside.

"Thank you for coming," Mr. McIntyre said, rising from Naomi's bedside. He let her fingers slip from his and nodded at Hope. "I'll leave her in your capable hands. I assume Lane is with you?"

"Yes, he's putting the horse up." She sat down beside Naomi and touched her forehead. The patient was flushed, a slight line of perspiration appeared above her upper lip. "How are you feeling? How far apart are the contractions?"

"About ten minutes." Naomi shifted, tried to sit up a little more. "And aside from this terrible, gut-wrenching ache that hits me every few minutes, I'm all right."

At first, Hope missed the humor, so focused was she on Naomi's well-being, but then she chuckled. "You're in good spirits. That's wonderful."

For the first time, Hope saw fear glimmering in the woman's eyes as she asked, "Are Hannah and Rebecca coming?"

"I asked Edward to inform them of the situation. However, it is snowing quite heavily. I wouldn't expect them 'til the morning."

"Then it's just you and me?"

Hope took her hand and squeezed it. "Naomi, it's going to be all right. You're in good health. We've monitored you and the baby as much as possible. I have every reason to believe the Lord is going to bless you with a beautiful, healthy child."

*A*nd while Naomi's labor did prove to be long and grueling, as first births often are, Hope was delighted at sunrise to place a perfect little boy in the arms of his mother. Naomi did not weep at the precious gift, but love emanated from her like rays from a summer sun.

She cradled him, caressed his cheek, gazed at him adoringly. "Is he all right?"

"Ten fingers and toes," Hope said, tucking the quilt more securely around the pair. "I'd like to get some more wood on that fire." The beautiful hearth had maintained a fire well and long, but now the flames needed fuel to keep the temperature comfortable for the patients. "And I'll, of course, let the father know he can come in now."

Hope took a moment in the hallway to savor privately the joy of bringing a baby into the world. A textbook birth except for one moment when she'd feared the umbilical cord had looped around the infant's neck. Following procedures for such an instance, Hope had kept her head and worked out the issue, praying all the while. Now, all was well. *Thank You, Jesus!*

Abruptly, her spirits sagged. Yes, working with children did seem to make so much sense. Patients her size, as it were. She imagined herself walking the halls of St. Bartholomew's, checking in on her little patients. In time, she supposed, Defiance and these people here whom she'd come to treasure would fade. As all memories do.

She suspected, however, a certain ache may never go away...

———

*L*ane couldn't help himself. That little, pink-cheeked cherub in Naomi's arms had him grinning like a mule eating briars. And then the lovestruck, dreamy expression on Charles' face as he gazed down at his son just about choked Lane up. Two men who had seen a lot of carnage in the war and more than their share of violence afterward—here they were all teary-eyed and featherbrained over a baby.

If that didn't beat all.

And he sure was glad for his friend. He slapped Charles on the back. "You did good, Johnny Reb. You did good."

"I think I had a little something to do with it," Naomi reminded him.

Charles reached out and brushed his wife's cheek. "You certainly did," he whispered.

Lane figured that was his cue to leave. He met Hope's eyes across the bed and she nodded at him. "I'll be ready to go in a moment. Naomi, I'm sure Hannah will be here anytime, and I'll be back tomorrow."

Naomi extended a hand to her and the two women clenched fingers. "Thank you, Hope. Thank you for coming to Defiance."

Lane didn't miss the way Hope stiffened. And he knew then, for sure, she was leaving.

---

*E*motions roiled in Lane as he drove Hope back to Defiance beneath a somber, slate-colored sky. It sure matched his mood. He was sick she was leaving. But if he didn't love her, all this hurt would pass. And she'd go on to be a happy, fulfilled doctor saving little lives in Philadelphia.

"You know, we need doctors to deliver babies here, too." The words had bypassed his brain, leaping from his mouth, catching him off guard. Now why had he said a fool thing like that?

"Yes, we've just seen evidence of that." She stared at him, but Lane didn't look at her. They rode a mile in silence until she asked, "Why did you leave the other day without saying anything?"

He searched his heart, determined to find the answer. Not knowing his own mind annoyed Lane. And, yes, scared him some. "I don't...want you to leave," he said haltingly. "But I don't want you to stay if..." he trailed off, frustrated that putting the feelings into words was so hard. "If it's not what you really want. If it's not what will...fulfill you.

You've worked hard to become a doctor. You gotta go where that gift takes you." He puckered up like he was sucking on a lemon, but he had one last thing to say. "Edward's right. You would be good with children as patients, but not because of your *genteel* stature. Because of your big heart."

Hope took a deep breath, let it out slowly, then slid her gaze to the snowy forest around them. "Without me here—or, really, even with me here—you have no encumbrances. No entanglements. When you do find the right woman, when you are ready to settle down, I'm sure she'll be able to ride and rope and probably shoot a gun, too."

Hope, when a man is in love, really in love, he doesn't run from it.

The words skittered and crawled in Lane's mind like biting ants. He hated Edward for all but calling him a coward. Even a fop like him had the courage to tell Hope he loved her. A galling realization.

Lane jerked on the reins and brought the wagon to a stop, a sneer lifting his lip.

"What's the matter," Hope asked, looking at him and then at their surroundings as if she was missing something.

"Dang it, he's wrong, you know."

"Who? Edward? A moment ago, you said he was right."

"When a man is really in love, he does run from it. Because he's scared he's not good enough for her. That he won't be able to keep her happy her whole life, not just the first few years."

Out of the corner of his eye, he watched Hope try to say something, but nothing worked past her lips. Suddenly, she jumped from the wagon and stomped forward to the horse's head. Lane didn't know what to do. What was all that she'd been saying about a roping-and-riding wife?

Slowly, he slipped out of the wagon, shoved his hands

into his coat pockets and kinda ambled forward, too. Hope was stroking the horse's cheek but staring right through him.

"I don't want to marry another cowboy," he told her flatly. Hope didn't reply but the tiniest of smiles twitched on her lips. Lane rubbed his neck. Boy, the water was deep here. "You'd have to be sure, Hope. 'Cause as it turns out...it's—"

"Edward."

Edward? Lane grimaced. "What?"

"Look." She pointed at a rider coming.

Edward was riding a tall sorrel and posting with the English style of riding, though he was on a western saddle, popping up and down like a prairie dog. Lane exhaled heavily in disgust. *Nice timing.*

Edward waved and rode up to them. "Good morning. I was coming to relieve you, Hope, let you get some rest."

"Why? Isn't Hannah coming?"

"She'll be along and is planning to stay for a few days. I was merely popping in to check the patient and only staying if the situation required it. Is Mrs. Miller...?"

"Fine. Her baby boy is fine. He was born at 5:03 this morning, all seven pounds, fourteen ounces of him."

"Well, it doesn't sound like I'll be here long then. But I will stay until Hannah arrives."

Lane forced the muscles in his face to relax and raised a hand to motion Hope back in the wagon. "Well, we'll be heading on into town th—"

A rifle shot shattered the peace and Hope's scream echoed with it...

CHAPTER 14

*I*n the instant he heard the crack of the rifle and their horses reared up screaming, Lane covered Hope like a shield. Another shot thundered over them and Edward, fighting his panicked horse, went sailing from the saddle.

"Into the woods," Lane yelled, shoving Hope in front of him, trying to shield her from any more bullets. Edward scrambled after them, dodging his horse and the one hooked to the wagon. Terrified, they both bolted down the road.

"Keep low," Lane ordered as they struggled through knee-deep snow to hunker down behind a broad pine. Edward dove into the shadows behind them, taking cover behind another tree.

Lane's mind was moving at the speed of light. *Right all along.* Another shot thundered down on them and wood exploded from a tree near his head. *Being hunted. We were sitting ducks out there...*

Gun drawn, he whispered, "You two stay low and hidden. Don't come out 'less I tell you." His heart hammered with adrenaline, but his muscles were steady as an oak. Gripping the Colt with determination, he surveyed the forest across the road, looking for movement or at least the most likely spot for a sniper. The faint scent of gun smoke reached his nostrils, but the woods hid their attacker.

"Lane, why is someone shooting at us?" Hope asked, gasping.

"I'm not sure." And he wasn't *sure*, but he had a strong suspicion. He wondered again about the bullet in the corral fence and the rifle shot he'd thought he'd heard over the cracking ice. This, then, would be the third attempt on Lane. He would make sure it was the last.

He peered around the tree quickly. He couldn't see the horses, but doubted they had run more than a few hundred yards. He waited another few seconds, listening, but had the sense the shooter was gone, in retreat, probably so he could try again another day. Lane, however, was not inclined to allow it. "Edward, I'm taking your horse. Hope," he paused, "we're only about four miles from the ranch. If I don't come back—"

"You will." She said it firmly, as if God Almighty Himself had ordained it.

With a nod, Lane holstered his Colt, cut through the woods, moving from tree to tree, making sure his exposure to flashing daylight overhead was fleeting. Finally, he was parallel with the horses. The two animals grumbled at one another as if discussing the strange turn of events.

Lane surveyed the woods across the road, the ridge above them. A stand of pines could be hiding a sniper. He listened, though, and something in the air told him the man was gone.

Getting away.

Determined not to let that happen, Lane tromped through the snow, clambered down from the bank, and landed in a low squat near the wagon. "Easy girls," he said, holstering his firearm as he made his way toward them. They started but didn't bolt. Lane eased over to Edward's horse, swept the reins up off the ground, and flung himself into the saddle. Once more drawing his Colt, he kicked the horse hard. "Let's end this hunt."

---

*A*fter Lane left, Hope and Edward remained still and silent for several minutes. But she prayed over and over, *Oh, dear Lord, please keep him safe...*

Finally, after what felt like an eon, she looked over her shoulder. "Edward, are you all right?" He hadn't made a sound since the horse threw him. And he didn't reply now. "Edward?" She turned around.

Edward was standing beside a pine, staring at his blood-smeared hand with wide, dull eyes. "Oh, my."

"Edward!" She ran to him, dropping with him as he slipped to his knees.

"I believe I've been shot."

Hope flung open his coat. The left side of his shirt was soaked with blood. It dripped down his arm inside his coat and painted the snow in bright, crimson drops. "Let me see —" As she tried to tug his shirt open, he fell forward on her. She caught him, grunting at his weight.

"Perhaps you should get me to the wagon while I can still walk."

Hope's heart nearly stopped with an agonizing realization. The horse had bolted. "There is no wagon." Panic squeezed her, threatened to fog her brain. "The horses bolted." She shook her head. *Get ahold of yourself, Hope.*

Edward staggered to his feet and she helped, though she wasn't certain this was the best course of action. She needed to examine the injury. *Think like the doctor you are, Hope!*

"Perhaps they didn't go far," he offered, his words coming out slurred. "Lane said he was taking my horse."

"Look, let me see the wound. That's the first order of business." She let go of him and peeled out of her coat. Edward swayed a little but stayed upright.

He must have seen the concern in her eyes. "I'll be fine. I'm in your capable hands."

"Yes," she said, spreading her coat on the ground at the foot of a tree. "Sit here." She aided him to the ground and leaned him back against the tree. She then peeled his left arm and shoulder out of his coat, noting immediately the bullet hole in both the front and back of the garment.

"Clean shot." He licked his lips but didn't say anything else.

"Yes. That's good." The bullet had passed through the upper part of his arm, near the armpit. "Edward, it looks as if the axillary artery was at least nicked."

"Which is not good."

"Nicked is better than severed, but we have to get the bleeding under control."

He needed surgery to repair it and quickly. She stepped away from Edward, raised her skirt and removed her petticoat. Wrenching furiously, she tore it into three separate pieces and shoved them into his wound. Edward grimaced but accepted the pain.

"Now, hold those—"

"Against the wound. I am somewhat familiar with the concept of slowing the bleeding, Dr. Clark."

On the verge of shock, yet his pride was still quite intact. Amazing. Out of habit, she turned to reach—Hope gasped. Her bag. "Dear God, Edward, my bag is in the wagon." Fear sliced at her insides, but she took a deep, calming breath. *Oh, Jesus, help me. Calm me.* "I've got to go get the wagon. How far—?"

"Hope…" She looked up at him. He touched her hand. They both knew how serious this situation was. "I'll be all right. Go. Get the wagon."

She stood up, nodding. Nodding to the plan. Nodding to her determination. "I'll hurry."

"Yes," he said a little breathlessly, "I think that would be best."

His words galvanized her. She would not come back to a corpse. She clutched Edward's face and locked gazes with him. "I will be back and you will be fine."

CHAPTER 15

*H*ope trudged through the snowy woods down to the road and looked off in the direction the horses had run. She had taken a few steps into the sunshine when she suddenly wondered, *Is he still there, Lord? The man with the rifle?* She glanced back in the woods toward Edward. Her present danger didn't matter. His was more pressing, by far. Praying for protection, she hurried the best she could down the road.

Her skirt grew heavy with clumps of snow and her toes were going numb. Regardless, she kept up a ragged jog, trying to stay in the ruts passing wagons had cut. Her feet slid and shifted beneath her, the snow tugged at her dress, but she hurried on, persevering and praying. Before she'd turned the first curve, she'd broken out into a sweat and her toes were actually warming from the exertion. Nice for the moment, but not advisable in winter temperatures. Not that she had any choice.

Thankfully, after only about ten minutes she saw the wagon. The horse had wandered to an open area and stopped, as if waiting for a passing stranger to give it some direction.

"Oh, thank You, Jesus!" Hope cried.

She hurried up to the animal, who looked back at her with ears pointed forward expressing happiness at seeing a human.

"Good girl." Hope scanned the tack, making sure everything was as it should be, and then climbed up. With a deep sigh of relief, she turned back for Edward, refusing to think he wouldn't be alive and waiting for her.

She used the whip and pushed the horse as fast and as hard as she dared on the snowy road and was back with Edward, all told, in less than half an hour. "Lane was right, Edward," she said, dropping the beside him, "the horse hadn't gone—."

His eyes were closed, and his hand had slipped from the blood-soaked petticoat. Hope grabbed his wrist and check for a pulse. There, but weak. "Edward," she tapped him on the cheek, "Edward, wake up. Wake up." He roused groggily. "You have to wake up. You have to help me get you in the wagon." She checked his wound. The bleeding had slowed considerably but it was still steady. They had time, she thought, but not much at all. If the ranch had been any farther away—

Edward nodded like a drunk man, with his head down and eyes closed. "All right." He was like lifting a live but slippery newborn foal. His strength ebbed and flowed unpredictably. He swayed and stumbled. Hope sweated and groaned working him to his feet. When he leaned too much of his weight on her, she feared her back would break. Sweat trickled down her spine as they struggled crazily, drunkenly, through the snow. Oh, but praise the Lord, the wagon was now mere feet away. They were going to make it.

Then Edward lost consciousness and crumpled to the ground, his deadweight slipping through Hope's arms.

---

*F*or a moment, disbelief and hopelessness flooded her soul. So close to the wagon...

She dropped down beside Edward and tapped his cheeks, calling his name. When he didn't rouse, she hit him harder, finally shook him out of frustration. "Edward, you have to wake up, I'm not sure I can get you in the wagon."

But he was in shock from the loss of blood. Consciousness would most likely not return. Time was slipping away...

She had a choice to make. Leave Edward here and go for help at the ranch, or get him there herself.

Both options seemed to mock her, the lady doctor with her fears and her physical limitations. Her *genteel* stature. Edward was as tall as Lane and maybe a few pounds lighter, but nothing that would make much difference.

She had been trained in moving patients from a gurney to a bed and vice versa. Medical school had not focused much on moving non-ambulatory patients. This situation was definitely akin to removing wounded soldiers from a battlefield—

A memory plowed into her. As horseplay, her father had shown how he and others had removed unconscious men from the battlefield at Antietam. Hope couldn't have been more than ten or so at the time. Could she do it? She'd always been the victim, laughing giddily as her father lifted her on his shoulders.

She studied the three feet from Edward to the back of the wagon. It seemed a yawning chasm. One try. If she couldn't manage it, she'd ride straight for—

She was wasting valuable time now. *Do it, Hope,* she commanded.

I will strengthen you, a voice whispered. *And help you. I will uphold you with my righteous right hand.*

She rolled him over on his back, shoved his knees toward his chest, placed her foot on both of his, grabbed his right hand with her left, and snatched him forward with every ounce of strength her cold, small frame could muster. In an instant, Edward was perched across her shoulders. A primal yell ripped free from her as she forced her legs to move.

"Oh, God, help meee…"

And she knew she could get Edward in the wagon. Because she wasn't going to do it in her own strength. Slowly, she stood up like the phoenix rising from the ashes, half-groaning, half-growling with the effort.

Another visceral, wild roar exploded from her chest as she managed the last three steps to the wagon. She inhaled, summoning strength and courage from the Holy Spirit, and with one final, triumphant cry, flung Edward onto the wagon's tailgate. Chest heaving, she paused for only a second to marvel over the feat.

As she thanked God, and thanked Him and thanked Him, she situated Edward better, went back for her coat to lay over him, and then drove them back to the King M Ranch as fast as if she were racing devils from hell.

She spared a backward glance and another hopeful prayer for Lane.

CHAPTER 16

Whoever it was coming after Lane, the man had to know there was no hiding tracks in the snow. In this situation, a person was going to either turn and fight…or plan an ambush.

Lane had followed the trail for about a mile along the edge of an open valley, catching sight of the other rider only once. When the tracks turned sharply up into the wooded mountainside, Lane knew the man had made his choice.

Ambush.

So be it.

Lane dismounted, tied Edward's horse to a stubby evergreen, and crept slowly, carefully, into the woods, gun drawn. A thick growth of Ponderosa pines had kept the snow a little thinner in here. Rock outcroppings everywhere provided a lot of high ground from which to shoot. Crouching lower, Lane stopped to think about the situation. It was not to his advantage and he stepped behind a boulder. In the same instant, the crack of a rifle shot exploded in the woods and tiny, sharp pieces of rock glanced off his cheek.

That was a little close.

He dropped to his knees and snatched a quick, careful peek around the rock in the direction of the shot.

A flicker of movement?

The assailant was changing positions.

Lane flexed his fingers on the revolver. *Come on, come on... give me a little more...*

A branch moved unnaturally on a cedar thirty or so feet up. Lane decided to go on the offensive, moving swiftly toward the tree. Close to it, he stopped to listen. Sounds, maybe the soft padding of feet in the snow, came to him. His sniper days jumped to life within him with jarring clarity.

Move a little, listen, move again, be ready to take the shot. If only he had his rifle...

Finally, he heard heavy breathing. The man had stopped. Was waiting and watching as well.

Lord, when the gun smoke clears, I'd appreciate it if I'm the one left standing.

Lane peered through the branches of the cedar. Unnatural lines and colors indicated his target. He took a deep breath and stepped out from behind the tree. Instantly, the barrel of a gun was pointing right back at him. Behind it, a young, Hispanic boy in his early twenties with cropped, black hair and burning, dark eyes glared at him. For an instant, Lane saw the surprise and fear in his enemy's face.

Unfortunately, it switched to foolish bravado.

So, there they were, guns cocked and pointing at each other, murder in the young man's heart, resignation in Lane's.

"Señor," the young man said in a confident voice, "I am Juan Gabriele de Valdez. You know the name?"

Lane nearly cursed. Valdez's boy had come for revenge, after all. "Put the gun down, son."

"I have come to kill a rabid dog."

"Take a look at the situation. This Mexican stand-off ain't gonna end the way you think."

If only the kid would listen...

"All the Texas Rangers. Dogs. And I kill dogs."

"You're a man of your word, I'll give ya that. Your Abuela dragged you outta Swansboro by the hair and you were screaming bloody vengeance the whole time."

"Sí. I did not forget. La Abuela did not forget. Her grandson will avenge the murder of her firstborn."

So, the grandmother had put him up to all this? Now Lane knew where Valdez Senior had come by his predilection for murder. "Put the gun down and I'll let you live. I won't repeat the offer."

The boy smiled, an evil expression oozing hate and triumph. "I have killed five Rangers. You will be number six."

Inwardly, Lane sighed. No choice...the only reason the boy hadn't pulled the trigger yet was because he wanted to gloat. His pride would be the death of him. "You shoulda just pulled the trigger."

Lane fired.

* * *

Hope held her focus single-mindedly on Edward's surgery until the last stitch was sewn and the last bandage tied. Then she sat down beside his bed, stunned by the emotions and exhaustion threatening to sweep over her like a flood.

On the other side of the bed, Hannah picked up the bloody instruments and dropped them into the washbasin. Her sleeves were rolled up to her elbows, but some red splotches spattered them, as well as the front of her apron. "I'll take these and have Maria boil them. You should go lie down. You look like you might fall over any second."

Hope nodded, stunned how relieved she was, how joyous that at least this part of the day was over, but the exhaustion made moving, talking, arduous beyond belief. Still, she managed, "Any word on Lane?"

"Not yet."

She swallowed against her fear. "Thank you. Your nursing skills improve every day."

"I'll do in a pinch." She rested the bowl on her hip and bounced her gaze back and forth between Edward and her. "We are beyond blessed to have you, Hope. Believe that."

"Thank you." Hope literally did feel as if she might fall out of the chair.

Hannah must have seen her fatigue. She set the bowl down and led Hope over to a settee near the stove. "Lie down before you fall down." She tossed a crocheted blanket over her.

"You'll wake me when Lane gets here, or Edward needs anything?"

"I will."

A great sadness settled over Lane as the kid fell backward in the snow, a spray of red shooting out behind him. Some folks, he reckoned, were just destined to die young. This wretch had killed some good men and that was partly because he'd never had anything but bad people in his life.

Lane looked at the smoking Colt in his hand and thought, *But for the grace of God there go I.*

He'd killed a lot of men and knew there were times he could have just as easily been on the other side of the law. Except a few good men in his own life had helped keep him on the rails.

Family and friends made all the difference in a man's life.

His thoughts shot back instantly to Hope. He'd been on the verge of saying something to the woman he'd never really thought would cross his lips. The future, though, stared him in the face when he looked at her. A future he wanted.

His gaze shot back to the dead man. *Dang. I ain't invincible. What if he'd—and I never got a chance to tell her?*

Lane didn't know all the ins and outs of love. Didn't exactly know how it was supposed to make him feel. Ah, sure, he figured he could live without Hope if she decided to leave. But he also knew, very clearly and painfully, her departure would leave him changed—empty, less than whole.

Merely *dallying* with a gal didn't do that to a man.

CHAPTER 17

*H*ope awoke to a warm room washed in sunshine. She stretched, yawned, made her way over to Edward. He was sleeping peacefully. She touched his forehead and was gratified his body temperature was normal.

Voices outside drew her to the window. A group of about six men rode by. She recognized Corky leading them. Her heart went to her throat, however, when she realized one of the horses had a body slung over it.

Oh, God, please don't let that be—

A soft rapping on the door made her spin, a fist pressed to her mouth. But then Lane peered around the door and she nearly fainted with relief. Hope launched into his arms. Laughing, Lane welcomed her in a tight embrace and lifted her off the floor.

"I've been so worried about you." She kissed him, smashing his face between her hands and he kissed her back, laughing at her antics. "I was trying so hard not to worry so that I could tend to Edward—"

Lane's happy expression darkened. "What's the matter with Edward?" He set Hope down slowly but held on to her.

"You rode off before even I knew. He was shot."

Lane flicked his gaze over her head to the man sleeping in the bed. "Is he gonna be all right?"

"I think so. The bullet nicked an artery. Fortunately, the horse hadn't taken the wagon far and we were close to the ranch. I'll be watching him for the next few days."

"Dang." Lane let her go and strode over to Edward's bedside. "He took a bullet meant for me. I feel kinda bad about that."

It wasn't Lane's fault, of course, but Hope decided not to say anything. She was just glad both men were all right. She slipped her hand into Lane's and hugged his arm. She didn't know why someone had taken a shot at him, didn't know how that had turned out, but could guess. All that mattered was that he was here, alive and breathing. She could touch him and hold on to him. And never let him go. Never let him out of her sight. Irrational, she knew, but, Lord, she was so glad to have him back safe and sound.

Lane made a thoughtful *tsking* noise, drummed his fingers on his thigh, then turned to Hope and rested his hands on her shoulders. "I started to tell you something out there and I'm gonna get it said if it kills me."

"I'm the one who took the bullet."

Edward's weak, raspy voice brought Lane back around to stare at the man with obvious annoyance. "Dr. Pratt, I'm sorry for your current condition, but you need to hold your peace for a minute. In fact, it would be nice if you would stick your fingers in your ears. Are you able?"

A shaky, but amused smile danced on Edward's lips. "Just tell the girl you love her and be done with it."

"Do you mind?" Lane snapped.

Smiling broadly, Edward closed his eyes. "A thousand pardons."

"That's exactly what I'm gonna tell her and I don't care

who hears, but you need to quit interrupting." Lane whipped his head back to Hope, an annoyed crease in his forehead, but he exhaled, and it smoothed out. For her part, Hope knew her eyes were shining like stars, her breath had caught in her chest, and her heart galloped wildly. She swallowed, waiting. Was he actually going to say it…?

"I do." Lane nodded curtly. "That's the way of it. I love you and I wanna marry you, Hope Clark." He wilted a little and his voice softened as if realizing he sounded abrupt. "That was meant to sound determined. But I want you to keep practicing medicine, too. It'd be nice if you'd consider doing it in Defiance, but if your heart is set on the children's hospital, well, I reckon we'll work something out."

A baby's hungry cry from the next room gave Hope the final nudge. That, and getting Edward into the wagon, had convinced her she was capable of doing relevant work in Defiance. She smiled and touched Lane's cheek. "There are some smaller patients around here who need me, too."

"Are you sure? That's important. You've got to be sure."

"I never wanted to leave in the first place, Lane. I think I just let my failures blind me for a little while." The baby was still crying, and Hope heard something in it she knew she should check on. She huffed, a little exasperated. "Let me go —" she motioned, shrugged, stepped away, "I should check—"

"Go. It's all right." Lane smiled broadly. "Reckon I'll be here when you get back."

*onplussed, dog tired, Lane sat down next to Edward's bedside and just stared at the quilt for a moment. Peace flooded him. He'd said it. He meant it. She wasn't ever going anywhere without him. He was going to grow old with Hope Clark. He was going to wake up every morning beside her. If he'd let it, the thought could make him downright giddy.

Probably would if it wasn't for the image of young Valdez's brains' splattering on the snow. Lane hadn't wanted to shoot him, but believed there had been no way around it. God had given him a *gift*. He could kill a man when necessary and not second-guess the decision. But he always made mighty sure before pulling the trigger.

"I suppose I should thank you, as well," Edward rasped, peering at Lane with one eye open.

"For what?

Edward closed his eyes, took a deep breath as if gathering strength to speak. "I don't know if she could have gotten me in the wagon without your help."

Lane scratched his head. "I ain't been here more than ten minutes. I rode off, found Valdez…" he trailed off, decided to skirt around that. "Ran into Corky and the other men after that. They hadn't seen Hope or you. She was already on her way back here."

"Well, someone must have—how else…?" Edward opened his eyes and stared at Lane, his pinched brow expressing bewilderment. "She must have had help."

Lane shrugged. "I've seen my momma snatch a two-hundred-pound deer carcass across her shoulders and tote it home." He inclined his head at Edward. "Might surprise you what a woman can do when a loved one's in trouble." Charles was right. The girl had grit.

Edward's eyes widened for an instant, but then the surprise faded to a more remorseful expression: defeat. "Yes, I suppose she *cares* for me." He wiggled his jaw around for a second, finally shook his head. "But I believe that's all."

The two men locked gazes, but they understood the war

was over. This was the surrender. Lane accepted it graciously with a subtle, curt nod.

"*I*s everything all right?" Hope poked her head into Naomi's room. Naomi was giving pointers to Mr. McIntyre on how to hold the infant. But babies sensed fear, and stiff arms made them nervous. Biting down a smile, Hope strode over and touched his arm. "The most important thing you should do is relax."

"I told him that," Naomi said, "but he acts like he's holding a Ming vase."

"The boy is so tiny," he said, wonder evident in his voice.

"Yes," Hope agreed, readjusting his arms to cradle the babe securely, "but not so fragile. Like this." She shifted his arm a little higher. "Just make sure to support his neck."

Proper adjustments made, the child quieted almost instantly. "There," Naomi nodded in satisfaction. "You're a natural, Charles."

He didn't seem to hear her. This man, a mover and shaker —some had said even a killer—was cooing with delight over the angel in his arms. When he realized both women were watching and grinning like monkeys, he hardened his expression and took the child to the other side of the room. A moment later, he was making silly faces and odd sounds at the baby. Hope and Naomi laughed, but softly.

"Still feeling all right?" Hope asked.

"Yes. Compared to what I felt like in the middle of delivering little Adam there—trust me, I feel like a new woman."

"Just tired?"

"Just tired," Naomi conceded. Then she turned her head and looked at Hope with a quizzical expression. "And what of you? You don't look tired at all." Suspicion crept into her voice. "You look refreshed. Glowing even?"

"Lane's back. And he's all right."

"Yes. So Charles said. But…"

Hope was about to burst. She had to tell someone. Where was Hannah? Naomi would have to do. "He said he loves me."

Naomi exhaled and rolled her eyes. "Oh, praise the Lord. I was starting to think he'd never get around to it and let you ride out of Defiance."

Hope pondered that a moment. "What if that's what I want? To leave."

A little smirk tilted Naomi's lips. "Then you'd go. But if you're staying, Hope, it's because you want to. Some of it's Lane, but mostly it's you. And I'm so glad."

*H*ope went back to her other patient and was about to push the door open to Edward's room, but paused to take a moment to consider things. She felt— invincible? Powerful? Something about getting Edward in the wagon had impacted her belief in herself and the Lord. The scripture, *"I can do all things through Christ who strengthens me,"* wouldn't leave her. *I can make it here, Lord, because I'm not making it in my own strength anymore. I'm not afraid. And now I'll have Lane with me, too.*

She looked heavenward and smiled at the revelation that illuminated her heart. *I'm joyful, Father, thank You.*

CHAPTER 18

"*L*ane, I know you want to get some rest, but give me a moment." Charles was standing in the doorway to his office, hands in his pockets, a thoughtful expression on his usually devilish face.

True, Lane had been heading for the bunkhouse to clean up, maybe catch a little shut-eye. It could wait. He followed Charles into his office, and they sat down on opposite sides of the desk.

"Corky said you said it was Valdez."

"Yep, and he was just as mean and determined to kill a Ranger as he was eight years ago. His grandmother fed the fires, though. Kept the boy focused on avenging her son's death."

Charles shook his head, grimacing. "Well, once again you've put a bad man in his place."

Lane looked down at his hands. How else was a man supposed to react to the gift of killing?

"Lane," Charles leaned back in his chair. "Beckwith leaves tomorrow. Defiance cannot be without a sheriff. Wade does not want, nor is he suited to, the position."

"You sayin' you want me to take over?"

"I do not want you to. You are the best foreman this ranch will most likely ever have. However, I'm thinking of the town where my wife and children will visit, shop, attend school. Where our town doctor lives and works." He lifted his brows, as if making a pertinent point. "You not only shoot with unholy skill, you were a Texas Ranger. That alone will probably keep Defiance quiet."

Lane's first thought was the sheriff's pay would be quite a cut and he had plans now. Plans to build a comfortable life for a wife. Eventually his own spread.

"I suspected you may have some reservations," Charles continued, "so allow me to sweeten the deal. You'll be in town more, obviously. You'll be better able to keep an eye on…things, certain people. Plus, your salary will be what I'm paying you as foreman." Lane opened his mouth to protest the high pay, but Charles raised his hand to cut him off. "Furthermore, I'll sell you a hundred and forty-acres with easy terms and give you one hundred head of cattle in six months. Call it a bonus."

"That's mighty generous—"

"And, you can hire four deputies. Keep Wade or not."

"Four?" Lane whistled. "That's a deal. And, again, generous. Suspiciously so."

Charles screwed his lips up into a grimace, then shrugged a shoulder. "Possibly one fly in the ointment. Delilah is wintering in Ruby City. She has plans to show up here in the spring."

"Good Lord." This news almost made Lane rethink things. He rubbed his neck, the muscles tightening at the mere mention of the woman. The infamous madam was a handful, and probably two-thirds of the town would try to lynch her if she showed her face here. "What do you think she's up to?"

"The rumor is redemption." He dropped his gaze to his blotter and Lane wondered if his friend was pondering his own spiritual journey.

"Well, I reckon it's possible for anybody. Look at you. But you really think she's changed? And if she has, why come back here?"

"Guilt? A death wish?" Charles looked up. "Regardless, I wanted you to know."

Lane exhaled heavily. The offer on the table was mighty compelling, still.

"I know you like ranching, but you liked wearing a badge, too. This could be the best of both worlds. And set you up for future...plans."

True enough, Lane thought. "But what about you? What are you gonna do for a foreman?"

"Emilio will be returning March first. I thought between the two of us, we could make a cattleman out of him. So..." Charles splayed his hands out, waiting.

Lane cleared his throat. "Well, before I say for sure, I'd kinda like to see how it would go over with a certain party."

"Yes, Hope." Charles grinned. "By all means."

*L*ate that evening, in a quiet house, Lane and Hope sat together on the great stone fireplace, each holding a cup of coffee. And she told him where her heart and mind were, of the sense of joy and courage filling her now. "I was alone when I came here and intent on proving myself to everyone—especially me. But I was leaning on my own understanding. I truly have a relationship with Jesus, and I feel like I can move mountains, Lane."

He nodded and grinned, staring at the steam swirling in

his cup. "Edward thinks you had help moving him into the back of the wagon."

"Do you think I did?"

"Yeah." He shook his head. "Just not the kind he means."

"And you're all right with my faith?"

"Maybe I ain't even all that far behind you. You bring back so many of the things my momma talked about..."

He faded off and Hope decided to tread lightly here, let Lane come to his own conclusions. She strongly suspected his mother had planted all the right seeds. Life and death were things to be contemplated on this day. "I'm sorry you had to kill the young man who came after you."

"About that..." Lane took a deep breath, let it out slowly. "I don't enjoy killing. Never have. I knew soldiers and Rangers who did. Blood lust burned in 'em. Not me. When I pull the trigger, I'm sure I'm doing what I *have* to do. It's the only way I can live with it. The certainty is what made me a steady Ranger."

Hope laced her fingers in with his. "Life is an ugly, beautiful thing, isn't it? Death and birth. Laughter and weeping."

He cut his gaze to her, his warm, hazel eyes pools of desire a woman could fall into and never find her way out. "Charles wants me to take over as sheriff in Defiance. How do you feel about that?"

She thought about it for several seconds. "My knee-jerk reaction is it is dangerous, and you shouldn't put yourself in harm's way. But then...it almost seems as if you were made for law enforcement. Your uncanny accuracy with a gun, steady nerves, and strong moral character recommend you."

"So, you'd be in favor of it?"

No, she wanted to scream. *Ranching is dangerous enough.* Yet, she knew what she had to say. "I want you to be happy. I want you to fulfill God's purpose for your life."

"I don't mind wearing a badge. I'll like it better if you're gonna be around."

"I'm planning on it."

"Not much fine wine in these parts, and even less Shakespeare."

Hope set her cup down and turned to face him. Firelight and shadows danced on his face. She combed a straight, blond strand of hair back with the rest, then let her hand come to rest on his cheek. "We'll write our own sonnets."

Lane dropped his head, seemed to be thinking, so Hope waited. He set his cup down as well and then slipped to one knee. Hope gasped but bit her lip to keep silent.

"I never thought I'd have need of it, but if I'm gonna do this right, it seems appropriate."

She arched her brow, quite intrigued.

Lane took her hand and cleared his throat. "Love looks not with the eyes, but with the mind; And therefore, is winged Cupid painted blind. Will you marry me, Hope?"

She couldn't honestly say which astonished her more: the Shakespearean quote or the proposal. Regardless, she was elated. Grinning like a fool, she took his face in her hands, and whispered her own quote from the Bard. "One half of me is yours, the other half yours—" She kissed him on the left cheek, "Mine own, I would say; but if mine," she drifted her lips over his nose and kissed his right cheek softly, "then yours...And so," she finished with a teasing kiss on his lips, "*all* yours."

Lane pulled her to her feet and wrapped her in a desperate embrace, his hands grasping at the seams in her shirt. He kissed her long, deeply, breathlessly. "I'm gonna kiss you like that every day for the rest of your life."

She matched his passion, letting her thoughts and fears fly away, finally enjoying the peace and freedom of their future in Defiance.

*L*ane was literally astonished at the way Hope took to riding. She was like a different person for the second lesson. She sat straighter and stronger in the saddle as Nancy cantered around the livery's corral. Hope's balance was centered and more reliable. Not perfect, but half the battle in riding was confidence. She had either discovered some courage or *rediscovered* it. Lane thought the latter was more likely. She'd let Defiance and Edward show her the worst side of everything.

She had to see the best for herself—the adventure of living here.

He grinned and patted the air. "Bring her in."

Hope considered the order for a moment, and then promptly brought Nancy down from the canter to a trot to a walk, and guided the horse over to him. "I did much better today, didn't I? I feel so—"

"Confident. It shows. And Nancy senses it. I think we'll go outside the corral next time."

"I'd love to. I'm ready."

Yep, there was not going to be any holding her back.

Hope was gonna go wherever a patient called her. And Lane had resigned himself to it. The fact had turned him into a praying man.

But faith didn't mean she had to go around unarmed.

He helped her down and put an arm around her waist as she pulled Nancy behind them. "I've got something for ya in my saddlebag. Call it a pre-wedding gift."

"Oh, all right."

He freed himself and walked over to Rusty. Fishing around for a moment, he came up with an oblong box and waited to give it to her as she wrapped Nancy's reins around the fence. "This'll take a few lessons, too. But I know you're up to it." He put it in her hands.

"Hmmm. It's heavy." She pulled the brown paper from it and lifted the lid on what looked like a cigar box. Inside, a pearl-handled, nickel-plated .32 revolver gleamed in the afternoon sun. "Oh," she gasped, "It's lovely."

"Go ahead and take it out. It's empty, but the first thing you always do is make sure." He set the box down on the ground and showed her how to open the breech and look into the cylinder. "It's a light gun, easy to load, pretty accurate, and I'm gonna make sure every man in the territory knows you know how to use it. Because you're going to know how to use it well."

She looked up at him, am impish grin flirting on her lips. "Yes, I will." She stroked the gun. "I will practice every day—" She squinted a little and brought the revolver closer. "What's this?"

"Read it," he said, not even trying to hide his delight over the perfect quote on the barrel.

She turned it more directly to the light. "Though she be but...little," her own grin grew, "she is fierce. A Midsummer's Night Dream."

"Act 3, Scene 2 didn't fit."

She raised her chin. "I'll treasure it and learn to shoot it so well, ruffians everywhere will fear me."

"I've no doubt of that, my darlin' doctor, no doubt."

*D*ear Reader, thank you so much for coming along with me on another adventure in Defiance! I would truly, truly be grateful for a **review**, if you have a moment. Reviews mean the world to us writers. Thank you again!

PROLOGUE

Naomi anxiously watched her husband from her seat in the wagon. John leaned forward in the saddle to stroke Sampson's neck and assess the narrow road before them. Little more than a rutted mule trail, it sliced unevenly across a steep, treeless, mountainside. The high bank along the left battled to hold back crumbling, jagged rocks while the right side of the road stalked the edge of a stark, breath-taking cliff. The edge plummeted several hundred feet to the ground below and then rolled into a wide, yawning valley surrounded by towering, snow-tipped mountains.

Truly a magnificent view, but the cliff sent an icy fear slithering up Naomi's spine. The road was barely wide enough for a wagon; the wheels would be mere inches away from . . . nothing. What would they do if something went wrong? There was no room for maneuvering. She knew by John's hesitation he was thinking the same thing.

He turned and looked back at Naomi and her sisters perched together on the Conestoga, a deep V etching his brow. She tried a brave smile but realized she was choking the reins so tightly her nails were gouging into her palms. Perhaps reading her true feelings, John quickly traded the worried look for a mischievous smirk.

"You're not scared are you, wildcat? After all," grinning devilishly, he tilted his hat back and shot her a cocky wink, "you're a better driver than most men I know."

While she appreciated his attempt to encourage her, today his playful banter couldn't ease her mind. She *really* didn't want to make this crossing, but decided to keep her fears to herself so as not to alarm Rebecca and Hannah. By the looks of them, clutching each other's hands and staring at the ledge with wide eyes, they were scared enough already.

"Would you rather I take the wagon across?" John asked more seriously as a breeze rustled through his shaggy blond hair.

She bit her lip and pondered the request. Most likely everything would be fine. It was only five hundred yards or so. Surely they could make it across without any trouble. She looked out at the valley and saw a lone hawk drifting on the wind, peaceful and content. She took it as a good sign. "No, I can do this. I'm sure it'll be fine."

She finished the sentence with a glance at her sisters, looking for their confirmation. Rebecca nodded. "As long as we don't look down." But Naomi saw the trepidation in her eyes. Hannah nodded, too, though her gaze didn't leave the cliff.

Naomi circled her shoulders to loosen the stress and relaxed her grip on the reins. "It's not *looking* down that worries me," she muttered.

"Everything'll be fine, ladies," John promised turning back to the road ahead. "Slow and steady." He prodded Sampson and called over his shoulder, "Keep the reins slack, and the wagon smack in the center of the road." He and the horse ambled forward, carefully pacing the mules behind them.

After several slow, tense yards, John fell into an easy rhythm with the sway of Sampson's body and Naomi breathed a little easier, too. Yes, this wasn't so bad.

Cautiously letting go of her fear, she swung her eyes again to the majestic view beside them. Jagged, white-tipped mountains clawed the cloudless, azure sky; slender Ponderosa pines and perfectly reflective alpine lakes dotted the rolling green hills below. A distant river of shimmering, blue water snaked its way through the valley's heart. Above them, the hawk dipped and spiraled on the breeze, frolicking in the glorious playground.

Naomi savored the gentle July sun on her shoulders and thought, with a little satisfaction, how folks back in North Carolina were already basking in intense heat and humidity. She for one was happy to be cradled in these high mountains and wondered if they might find a campsite near that river tonight. The possibility of a bath was positively intoxicating.

More than happy to let such trivial thoughts draw her away from thinking about that ledge, Naomi absently noted the small rock outcropping ahead but paid it no mind. It wasn't intrusive enough to alter John's or the wagon's path. Instead, she appraised her sisters out of the corner of her eye and appreciated how the journey had agreed with them. Neither of the three much cared for bonnets and, as a result, they all had a little too much sun on their faces, especially their noses. Hannah's hair, like her own, had turned the color of wheat in late summer and even Rebecca's dark hair flashed hints of caramel. The ladies back in Cary would have been scandalized by their earthy appearance, worn calico dresses and lean bodies carved by three months on the trail— lean, except for the slight rounding of Hannah's stomach, that is.

Dirty faces and all, they weren't very pretty right now and Naomi couldn't have cared less. She was done worrying about what scandalized who. California was their chance to leave all that behind.

A clean slate was especially important for Hannah. No one there would know the *son* of a rich banker had led her on, lied to her, promised her the moon and then left her alone with a child on the way. No one had to know the *rich banker* had offered Hannah money to leave town and never contact his son. Of course, she hadn't accepted, but the handwriting was on the wall. Their lives in Cary were over. John's brother Matthew had been inviting them out to California for years. Unanimously, they had agreed to go west.

And what about Rebecca? Widowed seven years now, Naomi could see a change blossoming in her older sister. She held her head higher than she had in a long time and her shoulders were no longer slumped as if she was carrying a weight. Rebecca was done, too. Done with grieving, done with paying penance for having survived a fire that took her husband and her daughter. Done with living in the past. They were all ready to discover some new horizons. Hannah's scandal had at least brought that about and Naomi was grateful for small favors.

She almost sighed in contentment. She loved an adventure and as long as she had that man up there on the horse, she would be fine. John was her rock, her oak, her everything. With him, she would cross a continent and not think twice about it. She wished she could be in the saddle with him, his arms, the size of small trees, wrapped securely around her. Oh, how safe and wonderful she had always felt with him.

A rumble of thunder drew her eyes to the west end of the valley where a mass of black clouds were carving their way through the jagged peaks. Even that made her smile. She could curl up beside John in the tent tonight, listen to the rain, trace that wide jaw and those broad shoulders, and kiss that silly grin right off his face. Warm. Dry. Safe. Yes, indeed, she was filled with all kinds of hope for their future.

Apparently John's thoughts had drifted as well. Interrupting her musings, he hollered back to the girls, "That must be the Animas River down there. My map says it isn't far from here. How do y'all feel about trout for our dining pleasure this eve—"

Sampson didn't see the rattler sunning on the outcropping until it was inches from his head. Startled from its slumber, the snake coiled and struck out angrily. The thirteen-hundred pound horse neighed, jerking his head away from the fangs with a mammoth movement of muscle. John, nearly flung out of the saddle by the unexpected reaction, clawed for the saddle horn and tried to hang on with his legs.

At the horse's commotion, the mules snorted and jolted the wagon backwards. Rebecca and Hannah squealed in fear. Naomi tightened her grip on the reins and fought for control of her own spooked animals, yelling, "Whoa, boys! Whoa!"

Busy wrestling her team, she could only focus on the battle up ahead in snatches. Sampson attempted to bolt, but John clawed his way back into the saddle, grabbed the left rein and yanked Sampson's head around, trying to get the panicked animal to walk in tight circles. The snake rattled in fury again, throwing Sampson into another round of pawing, prancing, snorting terror.

"Easy, Sampson," John commanded. "Easy . . ."

But fear in prey animals is as contagious as a cold. Mindless panic gripped the mules. Naomi seesawed back and forth with the reins as the pair tossed their heads, whinnied in panic and side-stepped, rolling the wagon away from the hysterical horse but toward the ledge. One wheel went over and the wagon lurched, tilting hard and then sliding further back. Gasping, Hannah and Rebecca clung to the seat and each other with white-knuckled grips.

"Oh, my Lord!" Hannah screamed. "We're slipping!"

"Hold on, Hannah," Rebecca croaked. "Hold on!"

Gritting her teeth and praying, Naomi jammed her foot firmly on the brake as she struggled with her team. "Whoa! Whoa!" she raged at the mules, sweat breaking out on her lip as she yanked on the reins. Frantic to get the team moving forward, she released the brake and snapped the reins. "Yaaah, get on now!" Rock and sand made a grating noise as the wagon slid again, and tilted at a sharper angle, but the mules obeyed the snap and tried pulling.

"Jump," Naomi commanded her sisters but they didn't move. She couldn't worry about them, too, and their foolish hesitation incensed her. She yelled again, this time with fury in her voice, "Jump!"

Hannah and Rebecca flinched at her tone then leaped from the wagon as it bucked again. The mules couldn't get that back wheel up over the ledge. In front of them, John abruptly gave up trying to calm Sampson. He sprang from the saddle and raced toward Naomi's team. The mules, seeing Sampson rear and then run in the opposite direction, made an attempt to follow.

"Stay on 'em, Naomi!" John shouted, fear lacing his voice —his tone frightened Naomi even more than the cliff. She obediently whipped the reins again as he grabbed a mule's halter and whistled the plowing command to *pull*.

The mules strained forward again then backed up a step. Naomi quickly slammed her foot down on the brake to stop the backwards motion, snapped the reins and urged them forward, releasing the brake when she felt some traction. Working the lever was exhausting but she was determined not to lose the wagon without a fight. Suddenly more gravel gave way beneath the back wheel; the wagon bucked and jumped as gravity and the mules fought it out. Naomi heard Rebecca and Hannah shriek.

"Get off a there, Naomi!" John yelled. "Just jump!"

"Not yet," she cried, meeting his gaze. They couldn't lose everything. "Not yet!"

Not wasting time to argue, John cut the air with another whistle, this one much louder and longer. Naomi slapped the reins again as John pulled on the mule's halter. Sampson came running back at his master's call, eyes wide, nostrils flaring, reins twitching and jumping on the ground like live snakes.

John gathered the reins, tied them quickly to the yoke then grabbed Sampson's halter. "Yah, back," he yelled, coaxing Sampson to pull. Naomi popped the reins hard across the mules' backs, praying to God Sampson would be strong enough to get the wheel back up on the road. The strain was tremendous; the mule's legs quivered with the exertion. "Yah, come on now, mules!" She barked.

John switched from Sampson to the mule closest to the ledge. He yelled, "Gee, Gee," while pushing the mules forward but away from the ledge. The wagon jumped and bucked again as it tried to crown the road. The path was so narrow John had to work with the mules and Sampson mere inches from the ledge. "Almost, Naomi! We're almost there!" She could see the veins bulging on John's neck as he pulled the mule forward.

She felt the tension on the wagon and the mules. Sampson was straining using his massive bulk to pull backwards; his leather reins looked as tight as guitar strings as he tried to bring the team with him. She heard her sisters' voices lifted up in desperate prayer and added her own *Please, God, help us . . .*

At the moment the rear wheel jumped back up on the road, a cracking, shattering sound exploded from the front of the wagon. In a blur of a motion, the mule closest to the ledge and Sampson broke apart; half the yoke hung from the mule's harness and it swung round like a hammer, catching John on the side of the head. Naomi saw in a split second the look in his eyes he knew what was coming, but there was no stopping it. He and the mule, loosed so suddenly from the wagon tongue and harness, simply launched like projectiles over the ledge.

John reached out for her but before she could even react, he disappeared over the ledge.

She heard her sisters scream. Or was that her? She heard the mule's panicked, desperate braying and then . . . silence.

CHAPTER ONE

Charles McIntyre stared placidly at his cards and stifled a yawn. He had not expected young Isaac Whicker to present such an entertaining challenge. Their little game had started at three and at seven they were still playing, though in a nearly empty saloon. This was the calm before the Saturday night gale.

Absently noting the low rumble of thunder, McIntyre decided it was time to finish the game. He had better things to do. Glancing across the table at his sallow-looking, gangly opponent, he could see the boy swaying and blinking as he fought against the effects of the whiskey. Hunched bleary-eyed over his cards, Whicker had fought surprisingly well to keep from losing his mercantile, but he'd never really stood a chance. McIntyre needed the store back and would have it back if he had to crush Isaac Whicker like a bug to get it.

Ironically, he realized, that wasn't the best way to start this new venture of making Defiance *respectable*, as the railroad gents had termed it. A lawless town would be a track-less town, they warned. Fine. Get a few legitimate businesses running, calm the town down, put a nice hotel where the mercantile is. Then the great American iron horse would come steaming into Defiance, bringing with it opportunity, success and wealth. Not to mention, carrying his gold away to the mint in Denver.

Oh, he knew he could simply bribe the right people, grease the wheels as it were, but he preferred to seek that as a last option. He even had the funds now to build his own railroad, if he desired, but McIntyre liked his money right where it was—in his own pockets. For the time being, he'd decided to take the easy road.

Ending the game with more boredom than ceremony, he laid down his cards. A royal flush. He heard Whicker's breath catch and looked up. The boy had turned impossibly pale and his blond hair looked suddenly dull and lifeless, like that of an eighty-year-old man. The tiniest speck of compassion attempted to make itself known to McIntyre, but he irritably flicked it away like a greasy crumb on his silk vest.

Scratching his thin, black, and perfectly trimmed beard, he leaned back in his chair. "Unless you can beat that, I own the mercantile."

Whicker shook his head and slowly placed his cards face down on the table. "No," he whispered, "I don't reckon I can."

Satisfied that was an admission of surrender, McIntyre rose to his feet. This game was over and he was ready to spend some time with the intoxicating Rose catnapping in his bed. "You played a good game, Whicker," he drawled in a deceptively charming Georgia accent. "The best I've had in some time, but you were destined to lose. I'll give you forty-eight hours to clear out. As we agreed, the inventory and gold stake are mine. You may keep all of your personal effects, including the wagon and your horse."

That last was overly generous, but taking a man's horse was just plain mean and McIntyre did not consider himself that callous–although he was quite sure Rose would have something to say about it. That feisty Mexican wench held on to things with the death grip of a mountain lion. Whicker replied only with a lingering blank stare. McIntyre concluded the boy was neither in a hurry to accept his fate nor leave the saloon.

Unwilling to be held up by the gloom in the air, he reached for the deed sitting forlornly in the middle of the table. "Let yourself out, Whicker, and have a safe trip back to . . ." *Kansas, was it?* He waived his hand dismissively. "Wherever you're from." Then he added generously, "You're an enterprising young man. I'm sure you'll be able to start over again."

McIntyre was almost surprised at himself for offering the words of encouragement and raked his hand through his black, wavy hair as if that would clear these dark thoughts. He supposed it was that accursed Southern upbringing which equated rudeness with horse stealing. In the cold light of reality, though, Whicker was nothing to him but an obstacle. Now an obstacle removed.

Well, nearly. The boy still hadn't moved. Sighing, McIntyre tucked the deed into his breast pocket and headed upstairs to his room. He paused ever-so-briefly at the top of the stairs to again flick away that crumb of compassion. After all, it had been a truly fair game. McIntyre hadn't cheated. He hadn't forced the boy to drink, nor had he forced him to bet the store.

Slapping the rail twice as if dismissing Whicker from his conscience, McIntyre strode across the hall to his room. Imagining a bath and Rose's heady kisses, he turned the brass doorknob and entered his room. From below, and barely above the soft thump of raindrops, he heard the boy mutter miserably, "Missouri. Hannibal, Missouri."

But the words were lost. McIntyre eyed the voluptuous

Rose seductively draped in his silk sheets and, undoing his tie, closed the door on Whicker.

―――――――――

In the dream, Naomi sat alone at the campfire waiting for her Guest. She tended to the fish in the skillet and kept a watchful eye. Shortly, Jesus joined her. He sat down on the other side of the fire and offered her a tender smile.

"Naomi, do you trust Me more than these?"

She was surprised to see that Rebecca and Hannah had joined them, too, though they acted unaware of her or Jesus. "Yes, Lord, You know I trust You."

"Then go where I send you." She put the fork down on the rock next to the fire and looked at Him, puzzled by His statement. Again He asked, "Naomi, do you trust Me?"

Her brow furrowed. "Yes, Lord, You know I trust You."

"Then go where I send you." She sat back and crossed her legs, puzzled, but sure there was more. Staring at her with dark, intent eyes, Jesus asked again, "Naomi, do you trust Me?"

She sighed, frustrated with Him. "You know everything; You know my heart. So You should know that I trust You."

"Then go where I send you. There are those around you living in defiance. Take to them the Good News." And then He pleaded softly, "Love them as I do."

"I will go where You send me, Lord." Her heart ached to ask one question of Him, though. "But can't You please tell me why You took Jo–"

Jesus put a finger to his lips, cutting off the question. His countenance and voice were gentle when He replied, "You'll have your answer in time. I have children lost in darkness. Take to them the Light . . . and don't stand on eighteen."

Naomi opened her eyes and looked up at the bottom of the wagon. A gray light crept stealthily upon them and she knew it was time to get moving. Slowly, gingerly, she climbed over her sleeping sisters and crawled out from underneath a home she now despised.

A lonely apprehension seized her as she wandered over to the dead fire. As she moved to sit on a fallen tree, she stopped short. Either Rebecca or Hannah had left John's map out, folded to reveal a small section. She picked it up and studied the lines and topographical details. John's accident had happened on what he'd called the Million Dollar Highway, the way most of the gold and silver was taken out of the valley. She let her finger dance over the map as she looked for something, some landmark or town, some hint of what to do next, where to go . . .

"Defiance . . .?" She stopped her finger at the town. The name tweaked her memory. "What . . .?"

But the Lord's words leaped to her mind: *There are those around you living in Defiance. Take to them the Good News. Love them as I do.*

She stared at the word. The town was only a few miles due west. She also knew, with a searing dread, that it was their destination. Feeling sick and overwhelmed, she closed her eyes and went back to her dream—now painfully vivid. She had told Him three times she would go where He sent her. *Not willingly*, she admitted. *Forgive me, Lord. I go grudgingly, to say the least. With John beside me, I would have gone to Hell and back. I had my heart set on growing old with him. Where didn't matter. Now nothing matters.*

The truth be told, Lord, I don't like You very much right now.

The admission broke her heart as much as the loss of her husband. If she didn't have the relationship with God that she had always counted on, then she had nothing. Yet, getting past her anger at this sudden destruction of her dreams was proving nigh unto impossible. She cried over her loss and her smoldering resentment and begged God to help her get past them both.

Get your copy of *A Lady in Defiance* to keep reading this thrilling saga, or pick up the *Romance in the Rockies box set*—which includes an unpublished novella AND footnotes—and save money on all the books!

ABOUT THE AUTHOR

"Heather Blanton is blessed with a natural storytelling ability, an 'old soul' wisdom, and wide expansive heart. Her characters are vividly drawn, and in the western settings where life can be hard, over quickly, and seemingly without meaning, she reveals Larger Hands holding everyone and everything together."

MARK RICHARD, *EXECUTIVE PRODUCER, AMC'S HELL ON WHEELS, and PEN/ERNEST HEMINGWAY AWARD WINNER*

A former journalist, Heather is an avid researcher and skillfully weaves truth in among fictional story lines. She loves exploring the American West, especially ghost towns and museums. She has walked parts of the Oregon Trail, ridden horses through the Rockies, climbed to the top of Independence Rock, and even held an outlaw's note in her hand.

She writes Westerns because she grew up on a steady diet of

Bonanza, Gunsmoke, and John Wayne movies. Her most fond childhood memory is of sitting next to her father, munching on popcorn, and watching Lucas McCain unload that Winchester!

I *love* to hear from readers. You can **find me** several different ways:
Receive a FREE book if you subscribe to my newsletter
Find me on Facebook:
https://www.facebook.com/authorheatherblanton/?ref=hl
You can also follow me on:
Bookbub and at
https://ladiesindefiance.com
I'd also like to cordially invite you to join Heather Blanton's Readers Group! You're welcome any time!

I love **Skyping** with book clubs and homeschool and church groups. You can always **email me** directly
at heatherblanton@ladiesindefiance.com to set up a time! Thanks for reading! Blessings!

"I believe Christian fiction should be messy and gritty, because the human condition is ... and God loves us anyway."
-- Heather Blanton

ALSO BY HEATHER BLANTON

In the same way Jesus used parables, I try, through fiction, to illustrate a Biblical principle. I pray you'll consider following his example—and then the truth of His love will set you free.

I love to hear from readers. You can find me several different ways:

Please consider signing up for my newsletter at

http://bit.ly/HeatherBlantonNewsletters

to get the latest news on new releases, events, parties, and other interesting bits of history! You'll receive a FREE story for subscribing!

Find me on Facebook, Bookbub, Twitter and Instagram.

I love Skyping with book clubs and homeschool and church groups. You can email me directly at heatherblanton@ladiesindefiance.com to set up a time!

Thanks for reading! Blessings!

LOVE, LIES, & TYPEWRITERS

A cowboy with a Purple Heart. A reporter with a broken heart. Which one is her Mr. Right?

HELL-BENT ON BLESSINGS

"Though she be but little, she is fierce." Shakespeare

LOCKET FULL OF LOVE

Was her husband a traitor or a spy? A good man or a villain? The answer lies with the locket...

~Romance in the Rockies Series~the Box Set or...

A LADY IN DEFIANCE—Book 1

His town. Her god. Let the battle begin.

HEARTS IN DEFIANCE—Book 2

Men make mistakes. God will forgive them. Will their women?

A PROMISE IN DEFIANCE—Book 3

Choices have consequences. Even for the redeemed.

A DESTINY IN DEFIANCE—BOOK 4

Romances and rivalries are simmering in Defiance...

~Brides of Evergreen Series~the Box Set or...

HANG YOUR HEART ON CHRISTMAS— Book 1

He wants justice—some say revenge. She wants peace. A deep

betrayal may deny them everything.

ASK ME TO MARRY YOU— Book 2

Part I — Mail-Order Bride

Here comes the bride…and he's not happy

Part II — A Proposal so Magical

Sometimes, it takes a truly strong man to surrender to love...

MAIL-ORDER DECEPTION—Book 3

Secret identities lead to stolen hearts.

Can love survive the truth?

TO LOVE AND TO HONOR—Book 4

Faith. Honor. Love. Which one will he sacrifice?

~Timeless Love/Time Travel~

IN TIME FOR CHRISTMAS – A NOVELLA

Charlene needs a miracle. God has one waiting …

a hundred years in the past.

FOR THE LOVE OF LIBERTY

She couldn't possibly be in love with a ghost, a mere shadow from the past.

But what if she is?

GRACE BE A LADY

Act like a man. Think like a lady.

~Sweethearts of Jubilee Springs Series~

A GOOD MAN COMES AROUND—Book 8

She has a list of qualifications for her groom.

He doesn't measure up.

Made in the USA
Columbia, SC
30 August 2022

66359779R00098